THE BASKET OF FLOWERS

BLACKIE & SON LIMITED
16/18 William IV Street, Charing Cross, LONDON, W.C.2
17 Stanhope Street, GLASGOW

BLACKIE & SON (INDIA) LIMITED
103/5 Fort Street, BOMBAY

BLACKIE & SON (CANADA) LIMITED
TORONTO

THE BASKET OF FLOWERS

Christoph Von Schmid

BLACKIE & SON LIMITED
LONDON AND GLASGOW

BIOGRAPHICAL NOTE

———

Johann Christoph von Schmid was born at Dinkels-bühl in 1768. He studied theology and held several curacies and a position as Inspector of schools before becoming a canon of Augsburg Cathedral in 1827. He was a prolific writer and his work, which was mainly for children, includes grammar books, readers and a Biblical History. As well as this he published about fifty stories. *Das Blumenkörbchen* (*The Basket of Flowers*) is the most famous, and has been well known all over Europe since the mid-19th Century. The first translations into English were made from a French version by G. T. Bedell, an episcopal clergyman in New York. Other books by Schmid include *Little Henry*, *The Stolen Child*, *The Cake* and *The Pet Lamb*.

Printed in Great Britain by Blackie & Son, Ltd., Glasgow

CONTENTS

THE
BASKET OF FLOWERS

CHAPTER I

FATHER AND DAUGHTER

In a certain little market town in Guelderland, there lived more than a hundred years ago an upright and intelligent man named Jacob Rode. He had come thither as a poor boy to learn the trade of gardening in the gardens of the castle of the Count of Terborg. His many excellent qualities of mind and heart, the readiness with which he set about everything he was asked to do, and it must be added, the frank and kindly expression of his face, soon attracted the attention of the noble family he served and made him a favourite with all its members. He was in consequence called upon to do many little duties in the castle, and when the young Count, after finishing his studies, set out on his travels, Jacob was made one of his retinue. In the course of these wanderings young Rode saw many strange cities and was brought in contact with people of different countries and habits, being thus enabled to enrich his understanding by a great variety of knowledge. By mixing much with cultured people also, he learned both to speak well and to improve his manners, so that on his return to Terborg, he not only gave pleasure to those who knew him by the evident good use he had made of his opportunities for educational purposes, but also—and still more—by the fact that he brought back a heart and a mind unspoiled by their contact with the great world.

During all this time Jacob had given the most complete satisfaction to his master, and when they reached home one of the Count's first thoughts was how best to reward his servant for his diligence and fidelity; after some consideration he decided to offer him the stewardship of his palace in the capital, which was a position of great trust and importance. Jacob, however, had no desire to live in the gay capital; he had seen enough of cities, and sighed for a quiet, useful life in the country.

It happened that just at this time a small property belonging to the Count became vacant; it was just the kind of house Jacob desired, and he accordingly asked his master to let him have it. The Count, eager to reward his faithful servitor, granted his request; but he was more generous than Jacob could have expected, for he bade him enjoy the place rent-free so long as he lived, and in addition promised him as much corn and wood for his future household as would be required.

This to the humble-minded Jacob was a princely fortune, and enabled him to complete his happiness, so far as this world's goods are concerned, by marrying a virtuous young woman of Terborg with whom he had been in love before he went with the young Count on his travels. His days now were spent in perfect calm and content. He rose early and worked late, tilling and taking care of the little property which was his for life, and which consisted of a pleasant little house in the midst of a large garden, half of which was planted with fruit-trees, while the other half was laid out for vegetables.

After Jacob had lived many happy years with his wife, who was in every respect a most excellent woman, she was taken away from him by death. His pain at her loss was inexpressible. The good man, who was by this time getting old, aged visibly, and his hair grew daily whiter and whiter. The sole friend he now had in the world was his daughter; she was the only one left of several children, and at her mother's death was but five years old. She was called Mary after her mother, of whom she was in all things a perfect image.

Even as a child Mary was uncommonly pretty; but as she grew in years her piety, her innocence, her modesty, and her unfeigned kindness towards all she came in contact with, gave to her beauty a rare and peculiar charm. Her face was lighted up with a look of such indescribable goodness, that it seemed almost as though one looked upon an angel. Before she was fifteen years of age, she was able to take the entire charge of her father's house; and never was a home better cared for. In the bright little living-room there was never a speck of dust to be seen; the pots and pans in the kitchen shone as if new, and the whole house was a pattern of order and cleanliness. Besides attending to all these things indoors, Mary managed to find time to help her father with the work in the garden, and the hours she thus spent with him out-of-doors were amongst the happiest of her life. For the old man, who had enriched his mind with knowledge and wisdom, was able, by his instructive and entertaining conversation, to make labour a pleasure and delight.

Mary, who had grown up in the midst of plants and flowers, and whose world was the garden, from her earliest childhood manifested the greatest delight in flowers. Her father, therefore, each year procured for her a few fresh seeds, roots, and cuttings, and allowed her the edges of the beds in the garden wherein to plant them and watch their growth. This was the occupation of her leisure hours, and it was ever the pleasantest of employments. Each little plant was tended with the greatest care; its growth and development were watched with increasing interest day by day, until, when the time came for the flower to unfold itself, her anxiety to see what it was like would almost get the better of her judgment; but, being schooled in self-restraint, she would wait with patience, and then, when the bud at last burst and disclosed the flower in all its beauty, her pleasure was indescribable.

Often would Mary's father say when he saw her delight: "Yours, my child, is a pure and innocent pleasure. How many parents give more shillings for jewellery and gay dresses than I give pence for flower-seeds, and yet do not give their daughters one-half the pleasure that I give you."

What was more, for Mary fresh joys blossomed every month, yea, every week. Often would she exclaim in her delight: "The garden of the Castle itself can hardly be more beautiful than ours!"

It was indeed very beautiful, so beautiful that people as they passed by would stop and admire, praising alike the garden and the gardener. And children, as they went to and fro, could not help lingering and longing as they looked through the palings at the rich array of flowers; nor, if Mary happened to see them, did they often go away without a sweet nosegay to carry home with them.

The wise father, however, while rejoicing to see his daughter take so deep a delight in flowers, knew how to turn her pleasure to a higher purpose. He taught her to see and admire in the beauty and the manifold charms of flowers the unvarying goodness, wisdom, and omnipotence of God. He was accustomed to devote the first hour of the morning to devotion; and in order that the day's work need not be interfered with, he rose an hour earlier than his labour required.

He thought that life of little worth which could not afford an hour, or at least half an hour, from the day's toil wherein to approach the throne of the Almighty, and there, in silent prayer and meditation, prepare for and sanctify the labour that was to be engaged in during the day.

In the beautiful spring and summer mornings, therefore, he would take Mary with him to a little arbour at the end of the garden, where, amid the songs of birds, they could sit and look upon the garden, rich with blossoms and sparkling with dew, and upon a far-reaching landscape bathed in the golden rays of the morning sun. Here he conversed with her about God, who causes the sun to shine, and sends the fertilizing rain and dew, who feeds the birds of the air and clothes the flowers of the field in such regal beauty. Here he taught her to know the Almighty as the loving Father of all men—the Almighty Father who manifests himself to us in manifold ways in order to draw us to him and to win our love—but chiefly through his beloved and only begotten Son. Here he taught her to pray by kneeling with her and yielding up his soul in heart-felt prayer. These morning hours, thus spent, contributed greatly towards planting in

Mary's heart the seeds of piety and devotion.

Mary's favourite flowers were the violet, the lily, and the rose; and Jacob loved to point to them as emblems of the virtues most becoming to her sex. When she once, early in March, brought the first violet to him and joyfully called upon him to admire it, he said:

" Let the modest violet, my dear Mary, be to you an image of humility and of the benevolence that does good in secret. It clothes itself in the tender colours of modesty; it prefers to bloom in retired grots; it fills the air with its fragrance while remaining hidden beneath the leaves. May you also, my dear Mary, be like the retiring violet, avoiding vain display, not seeking to attract the public eye, but preferring ever to do good in quietude and peace."

One morning when the roses and lilies were in full bloom, and the garden appeared in its richest array, Jacob said to his daughter, as he pointed to a beautiful lily, which was beaming in the morning sun:

" Let the lily, my dear child, be to you the emblem of purity. Look how beautiful, how pure and fair it is! The whitest linen is as nothing compared with the purity of its petals; they are like the snow. Happy the maiden whose heart is as pure and as free from stain! But the purest of all colours is also the hardest to preserve pure. Easily is the petal of the lily soiled; touch it but carelessly or roughly and a stain is left behind. In the same way a word, a thought may stain the purity of innocence!"

Then pointing to a rose he said, "Let the rose, my dear Mary, be to you an emblem of modesty. More beautiful than the colour of the rose is the blush that rises to the cheek of a modest girl. It is a sign that she is still pure of heart and innocent in thought. Happy is the maiden whom the suggestion of a thought that is indelicate will cause to blush, as she is thus put on her guard against the approach of danger. The cheeks which readily blush will remain for a long time with their roseate hue, while those which fail to blush at the least indelicacy of thought will soon become pale and wan, and go before their time to the grave."

Jacob plucked several roses and lilies, tied them together in a bunch, and gave them to Mary, with the words:

" The lily and the rose, sister flowers as they are, belong the one to the other; both incom-

2   (916)

parable in their beauty, they are rendered still more lovely by being together. In the same way, my dear child, are innocence and modesty twin sisters of virtue and cannot be separated. Yes, God designed that modesty should be the constant and faithful sister of innocence, in order that it may be the more easily preserved from danger. Remain modest, my beloved daughter, and you will also remain innocent. May your heart be ever pure like the snow-white lily, and your cheeks will ever resemble the rose in beauty."

Among the many fruit-trees that adorned the garden there was one that was prized above all the others. It was an apple-tree, not much larger than a rose-bush, and stood by itself in a bed in the middle of the garden. Mary's father had planted it on the day that she was born, and every year it bore a number of beautiful golden apples. Once it blossomed earlier than usual and with unusual luxuriance. The tree was one mass of blossom. Mary was so delighted with it that she went every morning as soon as she was dressed to look at it.

Once, when it was in full bloom, she called to her father and said:

" Look, Father, how beautiful! Was there ever

such a lovely mingling of red and white? The whole tree looks like one huge bunch of flowers!"

The next morning she hastened into the garden to feast her eyes once more upon the tree. But what was her grief to see that the frost had nipped it and destroyed all its flowers. They were all become brown and yellow, and when the sun came forth in its strength they withered and fell to the ground. Mary wept bitter tears at the sight.

Then said the father:

"Thus does sinful pleasure destroy the bloom of youth. O my child, never cease to remember how dreadful it is to be seduced from the path of right! Behold in the example of the apple-tree an image of what would happen if you were to wander from the way—if the hopes your conduct hitherto has raised in my heart should vanish, not merely for a day or year, but for life—ah, then, how much more bitter would be the tears which I should shed over your lapse from virtue than those which now course down your cheeks! Life would have no joys for me; with tears in my eyes I should go down sorrowfully to my grave."

As he spoke the tears stood in his eyes; Mary

was deeply moved, and the words he uttered
made so profound an impression upon her mind
that she never forgot them.

Under the eyes of a father so loving and wise,
and amid the flowers of her garden, Mary grew
daily in stature and intelligence—blooming as a
rose, pure as a lily, modest and retiring as a violet,
and as full of promise as a tree laden with blossom.

Happy was the old man at all times to behold
how plenteously the fruits of his garden rewarded
his diligent toil; but with how much more happiness and content did he mark the gracious effect
produced upon the heart and mind of his beloved
daughter by his pious teaching and example!

CHAPTER II

MARY AT THE CASTLE

One lovely morning in the beginning of May Mary had gone into a wood not far from the house to cut some sallows and twigs of hazel, with which her father used to make pretty little baskets when the garden did not require his care. While thus employed she lighted upon a hollow covered with lilies of the valley. They were the first of the year, and in her delight she plucked enough to make two bunches—one for her father, and one for herself.

As she was going on her way home through the meadows she was met by the Countess and her daughter Amelia, who generally resided in the capital, but who, a few days previously, had come to make a short stay at the castle of Ter-borg.

Mary, as soon as she saw the ladies, who were dressed in white and carried green parasols, stepped politely on one side in order to allow

them to pass, at the same time curtsying respectfully, as was the custom of the time.

" Oh, what lovely lilies of the valley! Are they
already in bloom?" exclaimed the young Countess,
who loved these flowers more than all others.

On hearing these words Mary at once offered
one of the bouquets to each of the ladies. They
received them with pleasure, and the Countess,
taking out a richly-embroidered silk purse, was
about to give her money for them.

But Mary said:

" Oh, no, my lady, I cannot accept anything
for my flowers. Pray permit a poor girl, whose
father has received many kindnesses at the
Count's hands, to have the pleasure of offering
you this little gift without thinking of reward."

The Countess was pleased, and with a friendly
smile said:

" If you will, you may from time to time
bring a bunch of lilies of the valley to the castle
for my daughter. She will be delighted to have
them."

Mary promised to do so; and every morning,
as long as the flowers lasted, she carried a bunch
to the house.

Mary was thus brought much in contact with

the young Countess Amelia, who daily grew more attached to her, greatly admiring her natural good sense, her unvarying cheerfulness, and her modest and retiring disposition. She was, in consequence, called upon to spend many an hour in Amelia's company long after the lilies of the valley had ceased to bloom. Indeed, the young Countess made no secret of her desire to see Mary constantly with her, and even gave more than one hint that she would like to have her in her service.

The anniversary of Amelia's birthday now drew near, and Mary thought she would like to make her a little rustic present. She had given her so many bouquets that a desire arose in her mind to take her something different.

During the foregoing winter Mary's father had employed his spare time making ladies' work-baskets, and one of the most beautiful of them all he had given to his daughter. He had procured the design for it from the city, and had put his very best work into it. This basket Mary at length resolved to fill with the choicest flowers, and to give it to Amelia as a birthday present. Jacob willingly yielded his consent to this idea, and in order further to enhance the beauty and value of the gift he wove into the basket the letters of the young Countess's name and the crest of her family.

The expected day having arrived, early in the morning Mary gathered the freshest roses, the most beautiful white, crimson, and purple stocks, dark brown and yellow wallflowers, the richest pinks, and other flowers of the most exquisite colours. She plucked also some green branches full of foliage, and disposed the flowers in the basket, so intermingled with green leaves, that all the colours, though perfectly distinct, were yet sweetly and delicately blended. One light garland, composed of rosebuds and moss, was passed round the basket, and the name of Amelia could be distinctly read enclosed in a coronet of forget-me-nots. The effect of the fresh rosebuds, the tender green moss, and the blue forget-me-nots upon the white latticework of the basket was very beautiful. Indeed, so perfect did Mary's little present look as a whole, that the grave father praised her good taste with a contented smile, and said:

" Let it stand there a little, so that I may have the pleasure of looking at it a while longer."

Mary then went to the castle with her present,

which she offered to the Countess Amelia, adding the best wishes of her heart for her young
friend's happiness. The young Countess was
then sitting at her toilet. Behind her stood her
maid, dressing her hair for the birthday feast.
Amelia received the present with peculiar pleasure; and she could hardly find terms in which
to express her delight as she viewed the charming flowers so tastefully arranged in the basket.

"Dear Mary," said she, "you have robbed
your garden to make me so rich a present, and
as to the basket, I have never seen anything like
it in all my life. Come, let us go and show it to
my mother."

She then took Mary in the most friendly manner by the hand, and led her upstairs to her
mother's room.

"See, Mother!" exclaimed Amelia, as she
entered the room, "what a lovely present Mary
has brought me! Never have you seen so beautiful a basket, and where can one find such exquisite flowers?"

The Countess also was greatly pleased with
the basket of flowers.

"In truth," she said, "this basket, with its
flowers yet wet with dew, is really charming.

It equals the most experienced efforts of the pencil. It does honour to Mary's taste, but more to the kindness of her heart. Wait a little, my child," she said to Mary, while she made a sign to Amelia to follow her into the adjoining room.

"Amelia," said the Countess, "Mary must not be permitted to go away without some suitable return. What do you think it will be best to give her?"

Amelia reflected for a moment, and then said: "I think that one of my dresses would be best; and if you will permit me, my dear mother, I will give her that which has red and white flowers on a deep green ground. It is almost as good as new; I have worn it but once or twice. It is a little too short for me, but it will fit Mary exactly, and she can arrange it herself, she has so much taste. If it is not, therefore, too much, I will give it to her."

"Do so," said the Countess. "When you give anything to those of humble means it ought always to be something serviceable. The green robe with the flowers will suit the little flower girl very well."

When they returned to the room in which they had left Mary the Countess said: "Go now, my children, and take good care of the flowers, lest they fade before dinner. I want the guests to admire the basket also, which will be the most beautiful ornament on the table. As to you, dear Mary, I will leave Amelia to thank you for your present."

Amelia ran to her room with Mary, and told her maid to bring the robe. Juliette (for that was her name) stood looking at her, and said:

" Your ladyship cannot surely intend to wear that dress to-day?"

" No," replied Amelia, "I wish to make a present of it to Mary."

" Give that dress away!" exclaimed Juliette. " Does her ladyship, your mother, know that?"

" Bring me the robe," said Amelia decidedly. " Leave the rest to me."

Juliette turned, averted her face to hide her vexation, and then went away, her face burning with anger. She opened the wardrobe with a pull, and took from it the dress of the young Countess.

" Oh, if I only dared to tear it to pieces!" she exclaimed. " This detestable gardener's girl has already won some of the favour of my young mistress from me, and now she steals from me this dress, for it belongs by right to me when my mistress has done with it. I could tear the eyes out of this hateful nosegay girl. But I will be revenged."

Suppressing her anger, however, she returned with a pleasant smile to the room, and gave the dress to Amelia.

" Dear Mary," said Amelia, " I have had presents to-day much more valuable than your basket, but none which gives me so much pleasure. The flowers in this robe are not nearly so beautiful as yours, but I think, out of love for me, you will not despise them. Wear it for my sake; and give my kindest wishes to your father."

Mary took the dress, kissed the hand of the young Countess, and hastened home, her heart full of joy.

Juliette, jealous and enraged, continued her work in silence. It cost her many a struggle before she could finish dressing her young mistress's hair, but she could not totally dissemble her wrath.

" Are you angry, Juliette?" asked the young Countess.

" I should be very silly," answered Juliette, " were I to be angry because your ladyship chooses to be generous."

"That is a very sensible speech," rejoined Amelia. "I hope you will always feel as reasonable."

When she reached her father's cottage Mary was all eagerness to tell her good fortune. But Jacob was too prudent a man to take much pleasure in so rich a present. He shook his grey head, and said:

"I would rather you had not carried the basket to the castle, but it cannot be helped now. This dress is truly valuable as a present from those whom we so highly respect. But I fear it will rouse the envy of others, and, what is still worse, that it will fill your own heart with vanity. Take care, my dear child, that the latter, at least, does not befall you. Modesty and good behaviour are more becoming in a young girl than the most beautiful and costly garments. Remember the Bible says it is 'the ornament of a meek and quiet spirit' which in the sight of God is of great price."

CHAPTER III

THE LOST RING

Scarcely had Mary had time to try on her beautiful dress, fold it up carefully after doing so, and put it away in her box, when the young Countess, pale, trembling, and almost out of breath, hastily entered the little cottage. Mary wondered what could be the matter; but before she had time to speak, Amelia exclaimed:

"Oh, Mary, what have you done? My mother's diamond ring is missing, and no one was in the chamber but you. Oh, give it to me, quickly, or there will be a terrible to-do! Give it to me quickly, and then nothing more need be said."

Mary, as may well be imagined, became exceedingly frightened, and turned pale as death. "Oh, my lady," she exclaimed, "what can this mean? I have not got the ring! I did not even see a ring in the room; nor did I move from the place where I stood."

But all her declarations could not convince

Amelia, who continued to urge her to give up the ring.

"Mary," she pleaded, "I entreat you for your own sake to give me the ring. You know not how valuable and precious is the one stone it contains. The ring cost nearly a thousand thalers. If you had known that, I am sure you would not have taken it. You thought it only a trifle of little value. Give it to me, I beseech you, and all shall be forgiven you as an act of youthful folly."

Mary wept bitterly at this suspicion. "Truly," she said, "I know nothing about the ring. I have never ventured to touch that which did not belong to me, much less to steal it. My dear father has always taught me too well for me to do a thing of that kind."

At this moment the old man came in. He was at work in the garden when he saw the young Countess enter in such haste, and he returned to the house to see what was the matter; and when he was told he was so utterly overcome that he was obliged to seize hold of the corner of a table and sink upon a bench. When he could command himself sufficiently to speak, he said:

"My dear child, to steal a ring of this value

is a crime which, in this country, is punished with death. But this is only the part of the matter the least to be considered. Remember the command of God, ' Thou shalt not steal '. One such action not only renders you responsible to men, but to that God who reads the heart, and with whom all false denials amount to nothing. Have you forgotten the holy commandment of God? Have you forgotten my paternal advice? Did you allow yourself to be dazzled, and so to be led away by the splendour of the gold and the precious stone? If so, do not deny the fact, but restore the ring. That is the only way in which you can make good your fault, so far as it is possible to make it good."

" Oh, Father," said Mary, sobbing bitterly, " I assure you I have seen nothing of the ring. If I had even found such a ring in the street, I could not have rested till I restored it to its owner. Indeed, I have it not."

" See," the father continued, " this angel, the young Countess, who has come here out of love for you, to save you from the hands of justice; who means so well with you, who has just given you so valuable a present. She does not deserve that you should tell her a lie, and seek to deceive her to your own destruction. If you have the ring say so at once, and the gracious young Countess will, by her intercession, save you from the punishment you deserve. Mary, I entreat you to be honest and speak the truth!"

"Father," said Mary, "you well know that I never in my life stole anything, even of so small a value as a farthing. I have never even ventured to take an apple from a tree or a handful of grass from the meadow of another; how much less, therefore, could I take anything so valuable? Oh, believe me, Father, for I never in my life have told you a lie."

"Mary," again said her father, "see my grey hairs. Oh! do not bring them down with sorrow to the grave. Spare me so great an affliction. Tell me, before God, before whom I hope soon to appear, in whose kingdom there is no place for thieves—tell me if you have the ring. For your soul's sake I implore you to tell the truth!"

Mary raised her eyes, which were filled with tears, to heaven, and said in the most solemn manner: "God knows I have not the ring! As surely as I hope for salvation, so surely I have it not!"

Convinced now of the innocence of his

daughter, the old man said: "I do believe you have not the ring. You would not dare to lie in the presence of God, and here before the young Countess and myself. And since I now believe you to be innocent, I am easy. Be you also at peace, my child, and fear nothing. There is but one real evil in the world that we need to fear, and that is sin. Prison and death are as nothing to it. Whatever may become of us, even if all men should forsake us and turn against us, we should still have God for our friend, and he will certainly rescue us, and sooner or later bring our innocence to light. Remember what he says: 'I will make thy righteousness as clear as the light, and thy just dealings as the noonday'."

The young Countess wiped away a tear as she said: "When I hear you speak in this way, I also believe that you have not the ring. But when I again examine all the circumstances, no other explanation seems possible. You must have the ring! My mother remembers distinctly the very place on her work-table where she put it down before I went into the room with Mary. Not a living soul was there but her. That I did not go near the work-table Mary herself can vouch. While Mother and I were speaking together in the next room Mary was left alone; before and after her no one went into the room. After we had gone Mother closed the door in order to change her dress. When she had finished dressing, and wished to put on her ring, it was missing. Mother herself carefully searched the room for it. She took the precaution to allow no one, not even me, to enter the room until she had examined it thoroughly two or three times. But all in vain. Who then can have taken it?"

"That is impossible for me to say," replied Jacob. "May God support us in this severe trial. But whatever may be hanging over us," he said, looking up to heaven, "behold, Lord, I am ready. Give me but thy grace, O God! That will suffice."

"I return to the castle with a heavy heart," said the young Countess. "Was there ever so sad a birthday? And I see no end of the trouble to come out of it. My mother as yet has spoken to no one on the subject but myself; but it will not be possible longer to keep the secret. She must wear the ring to-day, for my father, whom we expect from court at noon, will immediately notice if she is without it. He gave it to her the day that I was born; and she has never ceased to wear it on each succeeding anniversary. She fully believes that I shall take it back with me. Farewell," continued Amelia, after a pause. "I will say that I consider you to be innocent; but who will believe me?"

She went out overwhelmed with sadness, and her eyes filled with tears. Father and daughter were so overcome with grief that they could not even accompany her to the door.

Jacob seated himself upon a bench, resting his head on his hand, with his eyes fixed on the earth. The tears chased themselves down his wrinkled cheeks. Mary threw herself at his knees, and said: "Oh, my father! indeed I am innocent of this affair, indeed I am!"

He raised her up, looked long and earnestly into her eyes, and then said: "Yes, Mary, you are innocent. Guilt could never wear so honest and truthful a look."

"Oh, Father," Mary added, "what will be the end of all this? What will become of us? If it were I alone who was to suffer, I could bear it; but that you, my dear father, should suffer on my account—that gives me more pain than all the rest."

"Trust in God," answered her father, "and

be not dismayed. Without his permission not a hair of our heads can be touched. Whatever may befall us it is all ordered by God. It is all therefore for the best, and for our good. What more can we want? Have no fear, then, but keep always strictly to the truth. However you may be threatened, or whatever promise may be held out to you, do not depart a hair's-breadth from truth, nor in any way wound your conscience. A clear conscience is a good pillow even in a dungeon. We may expect to be separated; your father, my dear child, will no longer be with you to console you. But do not let that trouble you; cling all the closer on that account to your Father which is in heaven. He is a powerful protector of innocence, and nothing can deprive you of his support."

While they were thus speaking the door was thrown open, and the officers of justice entered the room. Mary uttered a cry, and fell into the arms of her father.

" Separate them!" cried the chief officer, his eyes gleaming with wrath. " Put the daughter in irons and take her to prison. Let the father also be held in safe keeping." He then ordered that the house and garden should be carefully guarded, and that no one should be allowed to enter until he and the sheriff had had them thoroughly searched.

The officers seized Mary, who clung to her father with all her might, but they tore her from the arms of the old man and put her in irons. She fainted, and in that state was carried away. When father and daughter were taken into the street a great crowd had already gathered. The story of the ring had spread like wildfire through the whole village; everybody in the place seemed to have collected round the little cottage, and the most conflicting opinions were expressed as to what had taken place. Notwithstanding the kindness Mary and her father had ever shown towards all, there were many who were pleased to see them in trouble, and who put the worst construction on what had happened. The comfort which Jacob and Mary had acquired by dint of industry and economy had given rise to much envy.

"Now," said some, "we know where all these good things came from; we were never quite able to understand it before. If this be the method, it is no great merit to live in abundance, and be better clad than other people."

Nevertheless, the inhabitants of Terborg, for the most part, showed a sincere compassion for Jacob and his daughter in their trouble, and many a father and mother were heard to say: " Alas! what wretched creatures we poor human beings are! The best of us are liable to fall. Who would have believed this of these good people? But perhaps it is not as is thought. If so, may God bring their innocence to light! And even if they are guilty, may God be with them and incline their hearts to confess their sin and to amend, and thus escape the great misery that threatens them! May he in his mercy guard us all from sin, for without his help we are not safe for a single day."

Many of the children of the village were gathered together with the rest, and when Mary and her father passed, they cried and said: " Ah, if they are put in prison there will be no kind Jacob to give us fruit, nor Mary to make us presents of flowers. They ought not to do it."

CHAPTER IV

MARY IN PRISON

Mary was almost insensible when they took her to prison. When she recovered from her swoon, she wept, sobbed, wrung her hands, and remembering where alone comfort was to be found, engaged in prayer. At length, overcome with terror, overwhelmed with sadness, and exhausted from having shed so many tears, she threw herself upon her bed of straw, and a sweet sleep soon closed her heavy eyelids. When she awoke, it was already night, and the darkness prevented her from distinguishing a single object. It was a long while before she knew where she was. The story of the ring appeared to her as a dream, and at first she thought herself on her own little bed; she was consoling herself with that idea when she felt the irons upon her hands. Frightened by the noise of the chains, she sprang up from her bed of straw, and all the sad reality burst upon her mind.

" Oh, what can I do!" she cried, falling on

her knees, "but raise these fettered hands to thee, O gracious God! Oh, deign to look down into this dismal prison and behold me on my knees before thee! Thou knowest that I am innocent! Thou art the only help of the innocent! Save me! Have compassion upon me, and on my poor afflicted father! Oh, give him at least some comfort, even if I must feel a double share of sorrow!"

The recollection of her father caused a torrent of tears to flow from her eyes. Grief and pity stopped her utterance. She continued for a long time thus to cry and sob.

The moon, over which until then large clouds had thrown a thick veil, now shone forth in full splendour, and threw on the floor of the cell the shadow of the grated window. Mary could easily distinguish the four walls of her narrow prison; the rough stones of which they were constructed; the white lines of mortar where the stones were joined together; the little projection in the wall which served in place of a table; the earthen pitcher and porringer that stood upon it; and the bundle of straw which did duty for a bed. But notwithstanding these signs and evidences of her misery, Mary felt comforted as soon as the darkness had passed away; the bright moon seeming to her like an old friend.

"Do you come, lovely moon," she said, "to look in at me as upon an old friend? Oh, when you shone into my little room through the green vine leaves that festoon the window, how much more beautiful you seemed than now, when your pale rays fall through the iron grating of a prison! Do you mourn then somewhat with me? Ah, how little I thought I should ever see you in such a position! Do you look down also upon my dear father? What is he doing? Is he awake, and watching you in sorrow, as I am? Oh that I might see him for a moment, as you do! Could you but speak, O lovely moon! you might tell him how Mary is weeping and mourning for him." The poor broken-hearted girl was silent for a moment. Then she said: "Oh, how foolishly I have been speaking in my sorrow! Forgive me for these idle words, O most gracious Father! Thou, O God, seest into the prison where my father lies! Thou seest him and me! Thou seest into both our hearts! Thine omniscient help is not hindered by prison walls and iron bars! Oh, send comfort to my beloved father in his trouble."

Mary hereupon noticed with astonishment that the cell was pervaded by a sweet perfume. She had in the morning tied together a few half-opened rosebuds and other flowers that were left over from the birthday basket, making of them a little nosegay which she pinned to her breast. The perfume came from these flowers.

"Are you still there, you dear flowers?" she said, as she caught sight of the nosegay. "And must you also come with me to prison, you innocent creatures? What have you done to deserve punishment? Ah, sweet friends in sorrow, there is my comfort—that I have merited this punishment as little as you!"

She took the little bouquet from her breast, and looked at it by the light of the moon. "Ah!" she exclaimed, "when I gathered these rosebuds this morning in my garden, and plucked these forget-me-nots by the side of the brook, who would have thought that I should in the evening be lying in this prison? When I fastened the garland of flowers round the edge of the basket, who would have imagined that to-night iron fetters would be fastened round my wrists? So uncertain are all things on earth, that no man knows how soon his position may be changed, and to what sad events his most innocent actions may lead! Well may human beings find reason to commend themselves every morning to the protection of God!"

Again she wept. The tears fell upon the rosebuds and forget-me-nots, and glittered in the moonlight like dew. " He who forgets not the flowers, but refreshes them with rain and dew," she said, " will not forget me. Oh, most merciful God, instil comfort into my heart, and into the heart of my dear father, as thou fillest the cups of the thirsty flowers with the dews of heaven!"

Amid her tears she again thought of her father. " Oh, my good and kind father," she said, " when I look at this little bouquet, how many of your wise words about the flowers come back to my recollection!

" This rosebud grew amid thorns, so may joy spring out of my sorrows. Whoever had tried to unfold this rosebud before its time would have destroyed it. God, who created it, has ordained that its tender petals should open gently bit by bit, and should breathe forth their delicate perfume. Thus will he turn my sufferings to account, so that the blessings they are intended to develop may come forth. Therefore will I patiently wait until his appointed time.

"These forget-me-nots remind me of their Creator. Ah, thou gracious God, I will not forget thee, as thou assuredly hast not forgotten me! They are blue, these tender flowers, like the heavens above me; and in heaven is my comfort amidst all the world's trials and sorrow.

"Here is a sweet-smelling sweet-pea with its delicate red and white blossom! As this slender plant climbs up the staff, without which it would be creeping in the dust, and thus, as it were, joyfully blossoming, soars upon its butterfly wings above the dust of earth,—so will I cling to thee, O God, and rise above the stains and griefs of life!

"This mignonette more than all the rest diffuses its delicious fragrance through the cell. Sweet, gentle flower, even her whose hand plucked thee thou rejoicest with thy perfume. I will strive to be like thee. I will endeavour to feel kindly towards those who have torn me from my garden and cast me into this prison, although I did them no harm.

"Here is a sprig of periwinkle. It shows its fresh bright leaves even in winter, and in the most dreary days of the year gladdens us with the colour of hope. Thus it cheers us, and bids us hope on. That I will; even in this hour of deepest suffering I will not give up hope. God, who can preserve this little plant fresh and green amid the storms of winter, and amid ice and snow, he will also preserve me—amid the storms of misfortune.

"There are also a couple of laurel leaves. They remind me of the unfading laurel wreath laid up in heaven for all those who suffer patiently and heroically on earth. Oh, it seems as though I could see it now, surrounded with rays of gold—this glorious evergreen crown of victory! Ah, ye flowers of earth, ye are transient and fleeting like its joys, and soon wither and fade away. But in heaven above, after the brief sorrows of earth, there awaits us a blessedness and a glory which is everlasting and fadeth not away!"

A dark cloud now suddenly obscured the moon. Mary could no longer see her flowers, and a darkness that could almost be felt filled her cell. Once more her heart sank within her. But the cloud soon passed away, and the moon again shone as brightly as before. "Thus," said the maiden, " may innocence for a time be under a cloud, but in the end it shines forth again in all its brightness and beauty. In the same way, O God, wilt thou at last enable my innocence, upon which dark clouds of suspicion now rest, to triumph over all false accusations."

Comforted and encouraged by these reflections, Mary bowed herself in prayer, and then laid herself down upon her bundle of straw and fell into a peaceful sleep. A pleasant dream came to her in her slumbers, and soothed and calmed her still more. She thought she was wandering in the moonlight in a strange garden, situated in the midst of a rough wilderness full of gloomy fir-trees, but of surpassing loveliness and charm. Never had she seen the moon so bright and beautiful. All the flowers in the garden seemed to become more beautiful in its soft and tender light. Her father also appeared to her in the entrancing garden. The moonbeams lighted up his venerable countenance, which was now smiling and happy. She ran to him, and, throwing her arms about his neck, shed tears of joy, with which her cheeks were still wet when she awoke.

CHAPTER V

THE TRIAL

Mary was scarcely awake when an officer came to conduct her to the tribunal. She trembled at the sight of the dark room in which the court was held. The judge was seated in a chair covered with scarlet, and the clerk stood before an enormous table, black with age, which was filled with writings. The judge asked Mary a number of questions, and she answered them all as truth required. She sobbed and wept, but persisted in declaring her innocence.

" Do not attempt to make me believe what is impossible," said the judge. " No one but yourself entered the room—no one but you, then, can have the ring. You had better confess, therefore, that you have it at once."

" I cannot," Mary answered, weeping; " I cannot speak anything but the truth. I know nothing whatever of the ring. I have not seen it, and I have not got it."

" The ring was seen in your hands," continued the judge. " Will you deny that?"

Mary persisted that the thing was impossible. The judge then rang a little bell, and Juliette was brought in.

Juliette, in the fit of jealousy which the dress given to Mary had caused, and in the guilty design of depriving her of the favour of her mistress, had said to the people of the castle:

"No one else has the ring but that detestable girl, the gardener's daughter. When she was coming downstairs I saw her looking at a ring set with precious stones which she had in her hand. She was startled when she saw me, and put it out of sight. Her action struck me as being very suspicious. However, I did not wish to be hasty and so said nothing. Perhaps, thought I, they have given her the ring as they have given her so many other things. If she had stolen it, I knew it would soon be missed, and then it would be time enough to speak. I am very glad that I had no occasion to go into the Countess's room. Such wicked people as that hypocritical girl might cause suspicion to fall on other and honester people."

In consequence of these falsehoods, Juliette was summoned as a witness, and lest she should be caught in a lie, she determined to maintain it, even in a court of justice. When she was summoned, and the judge required her to declare the truth before God, she felt her heart beat quickly, and her knees trembled under her. But the wicked girl listened neither to the voice of the judge, nor to that of her own conscience. "If," she said to herself, "I acknowledge now that I have lied, then I shall be driven away, or perhaps imprisoned." She persisted in her lie, therefore, and, addressing herself to Mary, she said with effrontery, "You have the ring; I saw you with it."

Mary heard this calumny with horror, but she did not suffer passion to get the better of her judgment. She could not, however, refrain from weeping, and her tears almost choked her utterance. "It is not true—you did not see me with the ring. How can you utter so wicked a falsehood, and thus bring such misery upon me, who have never done you any harm?"

But Juliette, who considered her own temporal interest, and felt nothing but hatred and jealousy towards Mary, persisted in her accusation. She even repeated her falsehood with additional circumstances and details, and then was dismissed by the judge.

"You are convicted," said the judge to Mary. "Every circumstance is against you. Moreover, the chamber-maid of the young Countess saw the ring in your hands. Tell me now what you have done with it."

Mary still asserted that she had it not.

Then, in accordance with the cruel custom of those days, the judge had her whipped until the blood came. Mary screamed and wept and, with prayers to God for his support, continued to repeat that she was innocent, but in vain.

Pale, trembling, and torn with blows, she was again thrown into prison. Her wounds gave her great pain. Stretched on a bed of straw extremely hard, she passed half the night without sleep. She wept, groaned, and prayed to God, who at last sent her a sweet and soothing sleep.

The next day the judge had her brought again before his tribunal. As severity had answered no purpose, he endeavoured to draw from her an acknowledgment by mildness and flattering promises.

"You have incurred the penalty of death; but confess where the ring is, and nothing more shall be done to you. The stripes you have received shall constitute your punishment. You shall return peaceably to your home with your father. Consider well, and choose—it is between life and death! I wish to be lenient with you. What good will the stolen ring be to you when your head lies bleeding at your feet?"

Still Mary stood firm to her first assertion.

The judge, who had remarked how much she loved her father, continued: "If you persist in concealing the truth—if you will not spare your own life, spare at least that of your aged father. Would you see his head, whitened by age, fall by the hand of the executioner? Who but he could have induced you to tell a falsehood with so much obstinacy? Are you ignorant that his life as well as yours is at stake?"

So terrified was Mary at these words that she nearly fainted.

"Confess," said the judge, "that you have taken the ring. A single word, the simple syllable 'yes', and you save your life and that of your father."

The temptation was great, and for some time Mary was silent. It was a moment of dreadful trial. The thought came into her mind that she might say, "I took the ring, but I lost it on the road." But "No," she thought afterwards;

" no, it is better to adhere to the truth. It is a sin to lie. Let it cost me what it will, I will not depart from the truth, even to save my own and my father's life. I will obey thee, O God, and leave all in thy hand, confident in thy goodness and might."

She then answered in a firm but tremulous voice, " If I were to say I had the ring, it would be a lie, and though this falsehood should save my life, I would not utter it. But," continued she, " if blood must be shed, oh, spare the white hairs of my dear father! For him I shall be most happy to shed my blood."

These words touched the hearts of all those who were present. The judge himself, with all his severity, could not help being moved. He remained silent, and made a sign for Mary to be conducted back to prison.

CHAPTER VI

A MOURNFUL INTERVIEW

The judge found himself in great difficulty in coming to a decision. "To-day is the third day," he said, "and we have advanced no farther than the first hour. If I foresaw any possibility that the ring was in other hands, I should believe the young girl innocent. Such obstinacy at so tender an age is almost unheard of. But all the circumstances are too clearly against her. It is impossible that it can be otherwise; she must have stolen the ring."

He returned to the Countess, and again questioned her as to the most minute circumstances; Juliette was also re-examined. He passed the whole day in reviewing the testimony, and weighing each word that Mary had uttered in her examination. At length, very late in the evening, he sent to the prison for Mary's father to be brought to his house.

"Jacob," he began, "I am known to be a severe man, but it cannot be thrown at me as a

reproach that I ever intentionally injured anyone. You will believe, I hope, that I do not
desire the death of your daughter; nevertheless,
all the circumstances prove that she must have
committed the theft, and the law requires that
she must die. The testimony of the chamber-
maid puts the question beyond doubt. If, however, the ring were returned, and the damage
thus repaired, we might grant her a pardon in
consideration of her youth. But if she persists so
obstinately in her guilty falsehood, it must be
because, though young in years, she is old in
iniquity, and there is nothing to save her from
death. Go to her, then, and persuade her to return the ring, and I pledge my word that then,
and only then, she shall not suffer the penalty
of death, but shall be let off with a less severe
punishment. You are her father, and have great
influence over her. If you cannot induce her to
acknowledge her guilt, what can we think except
that you are her accomplice, and have partici-
pated in the crime? I repeat, if the ring be not
produced, I shall show no mercy."

"I will speak to my daughter as you desire,"
Jacob answered, "but that she has not stolen
the ring, and therefore cannot acknowledge her-

self guilty, I know beforehand. I will, however, do all in my power, and if she must die, notwithstanding her innocence, I esteem it a great mercy to be permitted to see her once more."

An officer was sent with the old man to Mary's cell; he set the smoking lamp upon the little stone table, upon which was an earthen plate containing the prisoner's supper, which was still untouched, and an earthen pitcher full of water. The officer then left the cell, closed the door, and left father and daughter alone together.

Mary was lying on her straw bed, her face turned to the wall, in a quiet doze. But scarcely had she opened her eyes and perceived the pale light of a lamp, than she turned over, and seeing her father, uttered a cry of joy, and sprang to her feet so hastily that it caused her chains to sound. Then, nearly fainting, she threw herself upon his neck. The old man sat down with her upon her bed, and pressed her in his arms; both remained for some time silent, and mingled their tears together.

Jacob at length broke silence, and began to speak as his commission required.

"Ah! my father," said Mary, interrupting him, "you at least cannot doubt my innocence.

Alas!" continued she, still weeping, " is there no one who does not think me guilty—no one, not even my father? Believe, dear father—your daughter is not a thief."

" Be calm, my dear child—I do believe you. What I have done is in compliance with the order I received."

Both again were silent. Jacob looked at Mary, and saw her cheeks pale and hollow with grief, her eyes red and swollen with weeping, and her long fair hair flowing dishevelled about her shoulders. " Poor child," he said, " God has put thee to a severe trial; but I fear—I very much fear the most cruel, the most dreadful is yet to come. Alas! perhaps the head of my young child will have to fall by the hand of the execu- tioner."

" Ah, my father," Mary replied, " I care but little for myself, but for your grey hairs. God grant that I may not have the added sorrow of seeing you suffer such a death!"

" Fear not for me, my dear child," said the father; " I am in no danger. But you, my child, are in great danger. I hope still for the best, but fear there is little chance of your life being spared."

" Oh," cried Mary, transported with joy, and without allowing her father time to finish, " if that is the case, my heart is relieved of a great weight. All is well! Be assured, my father, that I do not fear death. I shall go to God, my Saviour, and I shall see my mother also in heaven. Oh, what a happiness will this be!"

These words made a deep impression on the heart of the old man, and he wept like a child. " Well, God be praised," said he, clasping his hands—" God be praised for the submissive disposition I find you in. It is hard, very hard, for a man bowed down with the weight of years, for a tender father thus to lose his only child, the child of his love, and his only consolation here—his last support, and the joy of his old age. But," he continued in a broken voice, " Lord, thy will be done. Thou requirest a heavy sacrifice from a father's heart. But I bring it willingly. Take her to thyself. Into thy hands I commit her—my dearest on earth. To the everlasting care of thy loving paternal heart I commend her; in thy keeping she will be best. Ah, Mary, it is better that thou shouldst die innocent, even by the hand of the executioner, than that I should live to see you robbed of your innocence and fall into sin. Forgive me, my dear child, for speaking thus. You are still good, very good—worthy to be with the angels in heaven—while the world is wicked, terribly wicked, and everything is possible: even the angels fell. If it be God's will, then, that thou shouldst die, my child, be of good comfort. You die in your innocence, and that is the best way to die, even though it may be a violent death. You will be transplanted, like a pure white lily, from this rough world to your everlasting home in heaven!"

A torrent of tears for a time prevented Jacob from speaking more. But after a while he said: "Yet one word more, my dear Mary. Juliette is the one whose evidence has condemned you. She declared on her oath that she saw you with the ring in your hand. On her testimony you die, if you are to die. But you pardon her, do you not? You will carry with you no feeling of hatred towards her? Ah, my child, even in this dark prison, upon this hard bed, loaded with irons, you are happier than she is in the palace of her master, clothed with silk and lace, and surrounded with every luxury. It is better to die innocent than to live dishonoured. Pardon her, Mary, as your Saviour pardoned his enemies! Is it not true that you pardon her and accept all this affliction as coming from God?"

Mary assured him that she did.

"Now," said her father, who heard the officer coming to separate them, "I commend you to God and his grace; and if you are not to see me again—if this is the last time I am permitted to hold converse with you, my daughter, at least I shall not be long in following you to heaven; for I feel that I cannot long survive this parting."

The officer warned the old man that it was time to go. Mary wished to detain him, and held him in her arms with all her strength; but her father was obliged to disengage himself as gently as he could, and Mary fell insensible on her bed.

Jacob was again brought before the judge. As soon as he entered he raised his hands to heaven and cried out, almost beside himself, "My child is innocent—she is no thief. Before God I affirm it!"

"I would that I could believe so too," said the judge; "but unfortunately I cannot be guided by the protestations of yourself and your daughter; I must pronounce sentence according to the nature of the testimony, and as is prescribed by the letter of the law."

CHAPTER VII

THE SENTENCE AND ITS EXECUTION

As may well be imagined, all were curious to know what would be the issue of this unfortunate affair in which Mary was involved. Every well-disposed person trembled for her life; for at this time the crime of theft was punished with great rigour, and the penalty of death was often inflicted for the theft of a sum not equal to the twentieth part of the value of the ring. The Count wished for nothing so much as that Mary should be found innocent. He read all the testimony, and had many consultations with the judge, without being able to convince himself of her innocence, because it seemed almost impossible that anyone else could have the ring. The two Countesses, mother and daughter, begged with tears in their eyes that Mary should not suffer death; while her aged father, in his cell, spent days and nights supplicating the Lord unceasingly that he would make manifest to the world the innocence of his daughter.

Whenever Mary heard the jailer approach with his clanking keys, she thought that he was coming to announce to her that she was sentenced to death. Meanwhile the executioner was engaged in preparing the place of execution, clearing away the weeds with which it had become overgrown.

Juliette, when out walking one day, saw him engaged in this work, and she felt a sudden pain in the heart, as though it had been pierced with a dagger. Horror seemed to deprive her of her presence of mind; and when she sat down to supper she could touch nothing, and was besides so pale and miserable looking that everyone saw she was not in her ordinary spirits. She went to bed, but her sleep was disturbed, and more than once in her dreams Mary's bloody head appeared before her. Her remorse gave her no rest either day or night; but the heart of the wicked creature was too hardened to confess her falsehoods, and, by saving Mary's life, atone in some measure for the evil she had done.

At length the judge pronounced sentence. Mary, on account of her theft, and her obstinate denial of it, was pronounced deserving of death, but in consideration of her extreme youth, and her hitherto unblemished reputation, the sentence of death was commuted to that of imprisonment for life in a house of correction. Her father, who was considered to be a participator in her guilt, either as an actual accomplice, or through the evil training he had given her, was banished for ever from the province.

Their possessions were to be sold to contribute as far as they would go to the reparation of the loss which the Count had sustained, and to pay the expenses of the court.

The Count mitigated the sentence in that, instead of being sent to the house of correction, Mary was allowed to accompany her father into banishment. It was further decided, in order to spare their feelings as much as possible, that they should be conducted across the frontier at daybreak the following morning before people were astir.

As Mary and her father passed before the castle gate, conducted by an officer of the jail, Juliette came out. Seeing that the affair, contrary to all expectation, had taken a different turn from what she anticipated, the heartless girl, destitute of every good sentiment, regained her gaiety. It had seemed to her too hard that Mary should lose her life, but she had no com-

punction in seeing her driven into exile through
her wickedness. That, indeed, was just what
she wanted. She always feared that in the end
Mary would supplant her. This fear was now
dissipated. Her first aversion against Jacob's
daughter revived, and she rejoiced at her misfortune; in fact, her bad heart had again ob-
tained the ascendency.

A few days before, the Countess, seeing Mary's
basket upon the sideboard, had said to Juliette:

"Take that basket away. It brings to my
mind recollections so painful that I cannot see
it without distress."

Juliette had taken it to her room, and now
brought it out with her.

"Here," she cried, as Mary and her father
approached; "here, take your fine present. My
lady wishes to have nothing from such people
as you. Your glory has passed away with your
flowers, for which you were so well paid, and it
is a great pleasure for me to give you back your
basket."

She threw the basket at Mary's feet, re-entered
the castle with a scornful laugh, and shut the
gate with great violence behind her.

Mary took up the basket in silence, and, with

tears in her eyes, went on her way. Her father had not even a stick to help him on his journey. Mary had nothing but the basket. She turned more than a hundred times, her eyes wet with tears, towards her paternal roof, until it, the castle, and even the steeple of the church were hidden by a hill covered with trees.

When the officer had conducted them to the stone marking the boundary of the province, which was deep in the forest, the old man, over-whelmed with anxiety and grief, seated himself upon the stone, which was covered with moss and shaded by an aged oak.

" Come, my daughter," said he; and as he spoke he took Mary in his arms, joined her hands in his, and raising them to heaven, said: " Before we go further let us thank God that he has brought us out of the dark, narrow prison into the free air and into the sight of the beauti-ful sky, that he has saved our lives, and has re-stored you to my arms, my dearly beloved child."

Jacob raised his eyes to heaven, which could be seen clear and blue through the leaves of the old oak, and he prayed with a loud voice:

" Gracious Father in heaven! Thou only comfort of thy children on earth! Thou almighty protector of all who are oppressed! Accept our united thanks for our merciful release from bonds and chains, from prison and death. Receive our thanks for all the benefits thou hast bestowed upon us while in the place we are now leaving. How could we take this last look at our home—now home no more—without looking up to thee with grateful hearts? Before we tread the soil of a strange land we implore thy blessing. Deign to look down on a poor father and his weeping child. Take us under thy protection and care. Be our guide along the paths which I and my dear child may yet have to tread. Lead us among good people, and incline their hearts to have compassion upon us. Let us once more find a little nook on the broad earth where we may spend in quiet the remaining days of our pilgrimage, and then die in peace. I verily believe, although we know it not, that thou hast already prepared such a place for us. In this belief, and with perfect confidence in thee, we go on our way strengthened and comforted."

After both had prayed thus—for Mary repeated in her heart all her father's words—their hearts were filled with unspeakable joy, and with a courage glad and uplifting.

CHAPTER VIII

A FRIEND IN NEED

While father and daughter were still sitting under the oak, Anthony, the Count's old huntsman, came through the wood. He knew Jacob well, both of them having been in attendance on the Count during his travels. He had risen very early that morning to go in pursuit of a stag.

"Good morning, Jacob!" he exclaimed, when he perceived his old friend; "is it really you? I thought I heard your voice, and I find I have not been mistaken. Have they in truth banished you? It is very hard to be obliged, in your old age, to quit the home that has become so dear to you."

"As far as the arch of heaven extends," answered Jacob, "there the Lord is, and everywhere his watchful kindness overshadows us. But our country is in heaven."

"Tell me," answered the huntsman, in an accent of pity, "have they banished you just as

you are, without giving you the necessary cloth-
ing for such a journey?"

"He who clothes the flowers of the field will
know how to provide for us also," answered
Jacob.

"Even so. But you are supplied at least with
money?" returned the kind-hearted huntsman.

"We have a good conscience, and with that
we are richer than if the stone upon which I sit
were of pure gold, and belonged to us."

"But tell me," said the huntsman, "have
you really no money at all?"

"This empty basket at my feet is our only
earthly possession," Jacob replied. "What do
you think it is worth?"

"A florin," said the huntsman, looking per-
plexed, "or perhaps a dollar. But what is that?"

"In that case we are quite rich," Jacob replied with a smile, "if it please God to grant
me continued health and strength, and the use
of my hands. My father was a basket-maker,
and he taught me his trade besides that of gardening, in order that during the winter I might
have a useful occupation. This has done more
for me, and has provided better for my future
prosperity, than if he had left me three thousand

crowns. A good conscience, health of body, and an honourable trade are the best and surest riches that we can have on earth."

" God be praised," answered the huntsman, " that you are able to bear your misfortunes so well. It is the right way undoubtedly. You are fortunate, too, in possessing such skill as a gardener. But, tell me, where do you propose to go?"

" Very far," Jacob answered, " where no one knows us. God will guide us to a place."

" Jacob," said the huntsman, " take this stout stick. I brought it with me to assist me in climbing up the hill, which I find a little difficult; and here," he continued, drawing from his pocket a little leathern purse—" here is a little money, which I received in payment for some wood in the hamlet where I passed the night."

" The stick I will accept, and I will keep it in remembrance of a generous man," said Jacob; " but as for the money, it is impossible for me to accept it. If it is a payment for wood, it belongs to the Count."

" Honest old Jacob," returned the huntsman, " make your mind easy about that. The Count has already received his money. Some years past a poor old man who had lost his cow could not pay for the wood which he had bought. I advanced him the sum, and thought no more of it. Now he has extricated himself from his difficulties, and yesterday, at the moment when I least expected it, he returned it to me with thanks. It is truly a present which God sends you."

"Well, then," said Jacob, "I will accept it, and God will repay it to you in some way. See, Mary, with what goodness God provides for us even at the very commencement of our journey. We have as yet hardly passed the limits of the province, and see, He sends us our good old friend, who has made me a present of a walking-stick, and now gives us money for our journey. Before my prayer was well uttered it has been answered. Let us therefore be of good courage and fear for nothing; God will watch over us."

The old huntsman, melted to tears, then took leave of them. "Farewell, honest Jacob; farewell, good Mary," said he, extending his hand to both; "I always thought you honest and God-fearing folk, and I think so still. Do not fear: things will yet go well with you; honesty tells in the long run. Yes! yes! whosoever does right, and puts his trust in God, will not find himself deserted. Take that as a word of comfort for your way, and may God be with you."

The huntsman left them, and bent his steps towards Terborg. Jacob got up, took his daughter by the hand, and wandered with her along the high road through the forest—forth into the wide world.

CHAPTER IX

A GLEAM OF SUNSHINE

Mary and her father wandered on, day after day, until they had reached a distance of upwards of eighty miles from Terborg. During all that time, though they had tried hard, they had found no situation in which they could earn a livelihood. The little money which they had was nearly exhausted, and they knew not where to obtain subsistence. It cost them a great trial to solicit alms, but they were at length obliged to submit to it. They presented themselves before a great number of doors, but they met with scarcely anything but repulses, often accompanied by abuse. Sometimes they were given a small piece of dry bread, which with some water from the nearest stream constituted their meal. Now and again they received a little soup or some cold vegetables, and now and again some remains of broken meat or pastry. For many days they had neither bite nor sup of anything warm, and at night they were glad to be able to find shelter in a barn.

One day when the road along which they travelled led between hills and mountains covered with trees, and they had walked for a long time without seeing any village, the old man was taken suddenly very ill. He sank down, pale and speechless, at the foot of a hill covered with pines, on a heap of dried leaves. Mary was nearly overcome with anguish and terror. In vain she sought for a little fresh water; not a single drop could she find. In vain she called aloud for assistance—echo alone answered her. On whatever side she looked no house was to be seen. Although almost worn out with fatigue, she climbed to the top of the hill, in order the better to view the surrounding country. Then she discovered on the opposite side of the hill, and quite at its foot, a farm-house surrounded by ripening cornfields and green meadows, and completely shut in by the forest.

She ran down as fast as she could, and at length reached the house quite out of breath. With tears in her eyes, and a voice broken with sobs, she asked for help. Both the farmer and his wife, who were somewhat advanced in years, were good, kind-hearted people, and were deeply touched at the sight of the poor girl—her pale face, her tears, and her evident anguish of heart.

"Put a horse to the little wagon," said the farmer's wife to her husband, "and let us bring the sick old man here."

While the farmer went out to harness his horse and bring out his cart, his wife got ready a couple of eider-down beds, an earthen pitcher of fresh water, and a bottle of vinegar.

When Mary heard that the vehicle would be obliged to go round the hill, and that it was a good half-hour's drive, she hastened with the water and vinegar by the same path by which she had come, and by this means was soon at her father's side.

She found that he had recovered a little. He was sitting at the foot of a pine-tree, and was greatly rejoiced to see his daughter, whose absence had caused him some anxiety.

As soon as the farmer and his wife arrived they placed him in the wagon and conveyed him to the farm, where they gave him a neat little back room, with another room adjoining, and a kitchen, which were then unoccupied. The farmer's wife made him up a comfortable, nice bed. Mary was contented to lie in the couch in order to be near her father, so that he should want for nothing. Jacob's indisposition arose from weakness, occasioned by bad food, want of rest, and the fatigue of the journey.

The good farmer's wife withheld nothing that the house contained that could in any way refresh and restore the poor old man. She spared neither meal nor eggs, milk nor butter; even a few fowls were gladly sacrificed to make nourishing soup for the weak old man. Nor was that all, for after a day or two the farmer took to bringing in a young pigeon from time to time.

"There!" he would say to his wife, with a smile. "Cook that for him. Since you do not spare your poultry, I must do something too."

These kind people had been in the habit of going every year to a fair in the neighbouring village, but they agreed this time to remain at home, and to employ the money which they would have spent in procuring medicines and delicacies for the invalid. Mary thanked them with tears in her eyes. She thanked God, too, for bringing them to such kind and hospitable people. "Praised be God," she said, "there are kind people everywhere, and it is often in the most unlikely places that we find the most compassionate hearts."

Mary was constantly seated beside her father's bed ready to attend to his smallest want; but she did not sit there idle. She had not her equal for knitting and sewing, and in these employments she occupied herself with great industry for the farmer's household. She did not give herself a moment's rest. The farmer's wife was greatly pleased with her industry, and her modest and reserved demeanour.

By the great care which they had taken of Jacob, and by the excellent food which they had given him, he was so far restored as to be able to sit up; and, as idleness had always been insupportable to him, he began again to resume his basket-making. Mary, as before, gathered for him branches of willow and hazel twigs, and his first production was a pretty little convenient basket, which he offered to the farmer's wife as a token of gratitude.

He had exactly guessed her taste. The basket was elegant, but strong and solid; branches of willow, stained with deep red, and interwoven in the cover, formed the initials of the farmer's wife, and the figures for the year. The border was formed of green, brown, and yellow withes, representing a cottage thatched with straw, on each side of which was a pine-tree. This pretty basket was the admiration of the whole house. The farmer's wife received the present with great joy; and the allusion made to the name of the farm by the representation of the pines, it being called "Pine Farm", gave her peculiar pleasure. When Jacob felt himself quite recovered. he said to his hosts:

"We have been long enough a burden to you; it is time I should go and seek my fortune elsewhere."

"What is the matter with you, my good Jacob?" said the farmer, taking him by the hand. "I hope we have not offended you. Why, then, should you wish to leave us? You have shown yourself thus far so sensible a man that this seems hardly like you."

The farmer's wife was deeply moved, and as she wiped the tears from her eyes, she said: "Why not remain where you are? The year is already far advanced. Do you not see the leaves on the trees, how yellow they are turning? Winter is almost already at our doors. Do you wish to be sick again?"

Jacob assured them he had no other motive for leaving them than the fear of being troublesome.

"Troublesome!" exclaimed the farmer; "don't distress yourself on that account. In the little room there you are in nobody's way, and you earn enough to supply all your wants."

"Yes, indeed," added the farmer's wife; "Mary alone earns enough with her needle and her knitting; and if you, Jacob, are inclined to go on with your basket-making, you will find enough to do. Not many days since, when I went to the christening of the miller's child, I took your pretty basket with me. All the women who were there admired it and wished to have one like it. I will undertake to get you plenty of orders, if you like. You won't lack for work, I assure you."

Jacob and Mary consented to remain, and their hosts expressed sincere pleasure at the determination.

CHAPTER X

Jacob and Mary now settled themselves in their little lodging and began housekeeping on their own account. A few articles of furniture were got for the living-room, and such cooking-utensils as were requisite for the kitchen. Mary thought herself very happy in being able to prepare the repasts of her father, and they led together a life of contentment. While Jacob was making baskets, and Mary was occupied with knitting and sewing, they amused each other with familiar conversation. Sometimes they spent the evening with the farmer and his household, when all were pleased to listen to the old man's amusing and instructive stories and his genial conversation. Thus winter, with its storms, passed quickly and in the most agreeable manner.

Near the house was a large garden, which was not very well kept. The farmer and his wife had too much to do on the farm generally to be able to spare any time for the garden; and besides, even if that had not been the case, they were too little acquainted with the art of gardening to do anything with it to good purpose.

Jacob, therefore, undertook to cultivate it and turn it to the best account.

He had made the necessary preparations during the autumn, and scarcely had the warmth of spring dissipated the winter's snow than he began the work, in which he was assisted by Mary. They used to start work early in the morning, and they seldom left off until quite late in the evening. The garden was laid out in beds; the beds planted with all sorts of vegetables, and flowers such as bees love, and bordered with gravel walks. Mary allowed her father no rest until he had brought her from the village (where he was in the habit of buying the seeds of vegetables) rose-trees, tulip and lily roots, and various kinds of flower seeds. She cultivated the most beautiful flowers, and among them were some which had never been seen in this rough out-of-the-way place. The garden soon exhibited such an outburst of verdure and colour, that the valley, until now rendered gloomy with dark forest-trees, assumed quite a smiling appearance. The orchard also pros-

pered much better under Jacob's hand, and
brought forth richer fruit, as well as in greater
abundance. In short, the blessing of Heaven
was upon everything he undertook.

The old gardener had now regained his accustomed cheerfulness; and began again to enter-
tain and instruct Mary by his reflections on the
flowers, but without recurring to his old obser-
vations. He always found something new to say.

During the first spring days Mary had sought
for violets along the thicket which bordered
their rustic garden. She wished, as usual, to
offer the first bunch of them to her father. At
last she found some beautiful ones which had
a delightful perfume, and ran, transported with
joy, to present them to him.

"Good!" said her father, taking the flowers
with a grateful smile, "seek and ye shall find.
But listen," he continued; "it is worthy of
notice that this beautiful flower, the lovely violet,
delights to grow among brambles. In that we
may find a lesson that applies specially to us.
Who would have thought that in this dark valley,
all covered with woods, and in this old cottage
whose thatched roof is green with moss, we
should find so much happiness? But there is no

6   (916)

situation in life so thorny that some quiet joy may not be discovered hid among the thorns. Have always, my child, a firm trust in God, and to whatever adversity you may be exposed, inward peace will never forsake you."

One day a tradesman's wife came from the city to buy some flax of the farmer, and brought her little boy with her. While she was engaged in examining the flax, and in choosing and bargaining, the child, having found the garden gate open, went in, and immediately fell upon a full-blown rose-bush and began to pluck the flowers, with the result that he scratched himself terribly with the thorns. The mother and the farmer's wife ran out into the garden as soon as they heard his cries. Jacob and Mary also hastened to see what was the matter. The child, with his little hands covered with blood, cried passionately, and denounced the rose-tree for having deceived him by its pretty flowers.

"It is sometimes thus with us bigger children," said Jacob. "There is not a pleasure but has its thorns like this rose. We run to grasp them with both hands, and frequently are only made aware of our mistake when too late. One is led away by his love for dancing or for play, another by a weakness for drink, or other vices still more shameful. Then we begin to weep and lament like this boy, and to accuse the thing that has caused us harm, while it is ourselves that are to blame. Do not let us be led to act thoughtlessly because a rose is beautiful, but let us rather enjoy it in the way that it was intended we should. God has given man reason, in order that he may learn to use things in moderation. If he follows its dictates he will not yield blindly to every impulse, but will act in everything with wise caution and foresight."

One beautiful morning which succeeded a two-days' rain, Mary and her father went into the garden, and found the first lilies in bloom, looking very lovely in the rays of the rising sun. Mary called all the people of the house, who for a long time had been curious to see the lilies in bloom. They were in an ecstasy of admiration.

"How dazzlingly white they are! How pure and spotless!" exclaimed the farmer's wife.

"Indeed they are!" said Jacob with emotion. "Ah, if the consciences of men were as pure, what a pleasing sight it would be for God and his angels! For a pure heart alone can claim connexion with heaven."

"And how beautifully straight and upright it stands!" remarked the farmer.

"Yes, as straight as a finger that points to heaven," Jacob replied. "I am happy to see this flower in the garden. There ought not to be a garden in the country where the lily is not found. Obliged as we are continually to look to the earth for sustenance, we are sometimes apt to forget heaven. But the fair upright lily should teach us that in the midst of our troubles and labours we should do well to raise our thoughts towards the celestial kingdom, and aspire to something better than the best the earth can give. Every plant," he continued impressively, "even the tenderest blade of grass, has a tendency to grow upwards, and those that are too weak to rise by themselves, such as the bean, and the hop which we see in the hedge, entwine themselves about the first support, and so climb by the aid of another. It would be sad indeed if man, with his hopes, his aspirations, and his knowledge of better things, should alone of all created things be satisfied to creep for ever upon the earth."

Jacob was one day employed in placing young plants in a new-made bed; Mary was weeding at a little distance from him. "This twofold labour, my dear child," said the father, "should be the only occupation of all our life. Our heart is a garden which the good God has given us to cultivate. We should be unceasingly employed cultivating the good and uprooting the evil that may find lodgment there. Otherwise it will become a wilderness. But let us scrupulously fulfil these two duties, and to this end implore the assistance and blessing of that God who makes the sun to shine, the dew and rain to fall, plants to grow, and the fruit to ripen. Then will our hearts blossom like a well-watered garden, and we shall possess a paradise within ourselves."

It was thus that Jacob and Mary led an active and industrious life, mingling instructive conversation with their innocent pleasures. Three springs and three summers had glided away, and the happy days they had spent at Pine Farm had almost caused them to forget their past misfortunes. But when autumn returned again, and the mid-day sun cast longer shadows, while the last ornaments of the garden, the red and blue asters, bloomed, and the many-coloured foliage of the trees showed the approach of winter, Jacob's strength began visibly to decline, and he very often felt himself far from well. He, however, concealed his feelings from Mary, fearing to distress her; but his reflections upon the flowers became more and more of a melancholy cast, and Mary, who observed this change, felt it to the bottom of her heart.

One morning as she was looking at a rose which had blossomed late, and was considering whether she should gather it, a breath of wind touched it, and it fell to pieces on the ground. "So it is with man," said her father. "In youth we resemble a rose newly opened, but our life fades as the rose; scarcely is it matured ere it is past. Pride not yourself, my dear child, upon the beauty of the body; it is vain and fragile; but strive after the beauty of the soul—the adornment of goodness which can never fade."

One day, towards evening, Jacob ascended a ladder to gather some apples. He handed them to Mary, who put them carefully in a basket. "How cold," he said, "is the autumn wind that whistles over the stubble field; how it plays with the yellow leaves and with my white hairs! I am in my autumn, my dear Mary, and soon yours will follow. Try to resemble this excellent tree, which produces fruit so valuable, and in such great abundance, so that you may please the master of this great garden, which is called the world."

As Mary was one day sowing some seed for the following spring, her father said: "The day will come when they will put us in the ground as you are putting these seeds, and the soil will cover us. But console yourself, my dear child! As after a little while the tiny seed begins to stir in the earth, shows signs of life, and in the form of a fair flower raises its head above the ground, thus, as it were, triumphing over the grave, so shall we one day rise to a new and everlasting life out of the darkness of the tomb. Think of this, my dear Mary, when in the course of nature I am laid to rest; and when you see the flowers which you plant upon my grave springing up to renewed life in the spring, let them be to you an emblem and an assurance of resurrection and immortality."

Mary looked wistfully at her father. Two large tears stood in his eyes, and he seemed greatly changed. She knew that he was thinking of her, and that she must soon be left alone in a world of temptations and sorrows. Sad and painful forebodings filled her heart, and she fell down on her knees by his side and wept with him.

CHAPTER XI

JACOB'S ILLNESS

At the beginning of winter, which threatened to be very severe, and which had already covered mountain and valley with snow, Jacob became very ill. Mary begged him to allow the physician of the neighbouring village to come and see him; and immediately the farmer, who was always on the alert to do a kindness, drove over in his sledge to fetch him. The doctor wrote his prescription, and Mary walked with him as far as the door to ask if he had any hope of her father's recovery. He replied that the old man was in no immediate danger, but that his disease would turn to consumption, and that, especially at his age, he could not be expected to recover. At this intelligence Mary nearly fainted. She wept and sobbed, and could hardly be comforted. After a time, however, she became more composed, wiped away her tears, and endeavoured to appear calm before she returned to her father, for fear of distressing him.

Mary attended her father with all the care that a good daughter could bestow on a most beloved parent. She watched his every look in order to anticipate his slightest want, and every night was spent in wakeful solicitude by his bedside. If anyone wished to relieve her for fear that she should herself become sick, and if she, after much persuasion, consented to rest for a few moments on her couch, it very rarely happened that she closed her eyes. Did her father but cough, she trembled; if he made the least stir, she immediately approached him softly and on tiptoe to inquire how he was. With the tenderest love she prepared and brought him the food which best suited his condition. She arranged his pillow, read to him, and prayed for him continually. Often when he dozed for a little while she would stand by his bed with her hands clasped and her tearful eyes raised up to heaven, and sigh:

"Oh, God, may it please thee to spare him to me a little longer, if it be but a few years!"

Mary had a little money which she had saved from the work of her own hands. She had earned it by very often spending half the night in sewing and knitting. This she made use of to the last penny in procuring such delicacies for her father as she thought might tempt him to eat, and so tend to sustain his strength.

The pious old man, although he felt himself occasionally a little stronger, was only too sure he was on his death-bed. But he was calm and perfectly resigned. He spoke of his approaching death with the greatest serenity.

" Ah!" exclaimed Mary, crying bitterly, " do not speak thus, my dear father. I cannot bear the thought. What would become of me? Alas! your poor Mary would then not have a friend on earth."

" Do not cry, my dear child," said her father, holding out his hand to her; " you have a kind Father in heaven. He will never forsake you, although your earthly father be taken away from you. I do not feel the least anxious about the manner in which you will gain a livelihood; no, that does not distress me in the least. The birds of the air are supplied with food; why should not you also be provided for? If God cares for the smallest sparrow, surely He will likewise care for you, who are worth many sparrows! Man's wants are but few, and those for only a short time. No, so far as your mere material wants are concerned I have no anxiety; but it is different when I think of your spiritual welfare. If I could be sure that you would ever remain as good and pious and innocent as, thank God, you are now, I should die happy."

Mary sobbed, " Ah, Father, do not fear for me. I shall always think of you, and be guided by your instruction."

" Alas! my dear child," Jacob replied, " you do not suspect the world of being half so wicked or corrupt as it is, or of containing half so many wicked people as it does. It grieves me to say it, but it is only too true, that there are men in the world who would think it merely a jest to deprive you, my poor girl, of innocence, honour, peace of heart, and the whole happiness of your life. They would call you childish if you spoke of the fear of God, of conscience, the command-ments of God, and of eternity. My child, avoid such men! When they flatter you, and call you beautiful, and hover about you as the butterfly round the flower, do not listen to them or take any notice of what they say. Never accept a present from them, and place no trust in their promises. Under the form of an angel a very Satan is frequently hidden, and beneath the most beautiful flowers a serpent often sleeps. But God has given you for your protection that guardian feeling, modesty. If anyone suggests an evil thought, or even utters a word, in your presence that is inimical to innocence or good manners, you will feel the glow of modesty mount to your cheek. Take warning from this guardian of innocence. Do not neglect it, lest it leave you for ever. So long as modesty remains, and you listen to its angelic warning, you will not be led astray; but neglect its warning even for once and in the slightest degree, and you are in danger of being lost for ever."

Mary, deeply moved, pressed her father's hand.

" Ah, my dear child," he continued, " you will find even an enemy in your own heart. There will be moments in your life when you will feel a desire for what is evil, and when you may persuade yourself that it is not so very bad, or even that it is unsinful and permissible. But take warning, and let the words of your dying father be deeply engraven upon your heart. Do, speak, think nothing for which you would blush if your father knew what was passing in your heart. My eyes will soon be closed for ever; then I shall be able to watch over you no more, as I have hitherto done. But remember that your heavenly Father, who is everywhere and sees everything, is able also to read the secrets of your heart. You would be loth to trouble me, your earthly father, by falling into bad conduct; how much more then should you fear and strive not to offend your Almighty Father who is in heaven?"

After a pause the old man continued: " Look at me once more, Mary; I shall not be much longer with you. Oh, if you should ever be tempted to do wrong, think of my pale face, and of the tears which wet my sunken cheeks. Come to me, put your hand into mine, cold and withered, which will soon fall into dust. Promise me never to forget my words. In the hour of temptation imagine you feel this cold hand which you now hold, and which is on the brink of the grave. Poor child, you cannot see without weeping my pale and hollow cheeks. Ah! know that everything passes away in this world. There was a time when I too had the bloom of health, and the fresh and vermilion tint which you now have. The time will come when you too will be stretched on the bed of death, pale and emaciated as you now see me, if God does not sooner take you to himself. The friends of my youth have disappeared like the flowers which have passed away with spring, and for whose place you seek in vain, like the dew which but for a moment sparkles on the flowers, and is gone."

The next day Jacob, believing that his end was near, felt, though very weak, that it was his duty to continue his dying advice.

"I have seen the world," he said, "as well as other people, when I accompanied the young Count in his travels. Was there anything in the large cities superb or magnificent, I went to see it. I spent whole weeks in pleasure. Was there a brilliant assembly, or a lively conversation, I saw and heard all, as well as my young master. I always had my share in the most dainty meals, and of the choicest wines, and always had more than I wished for. But all these noisy pleasures left me with an empty heart. I here protest solemnly that a few moments of peaceful contemplation and fervent prayer under our arbour in Terborg, or under that thatch that covers us now, gave me more real joy than all— even on my death-bed I repeat it—more than all the vain pleasures of this world. Seek, then, your happiness in the love and service of our blessed

Saviour. You will find him, and he will bless you. You know very well, my dear child, that I have not wanted for misfortunes in this life. Alas! when I lost your mother my heart was for a long time like a dry and barren garden, whose soil, burnt by the heat of the sun, cracks open and seems to sigh for rain. It is thus that I languished, thirsting for consolation; at last I found it in the Lord.

"Oh! my child, there will be days in your life when your heart also will be like a dry and barren ground. But do not feel distressed at it. The thirsty ground calls not in vain for rain. God sends the rain necessary for it. Seek your consolation in the Lord. This consolation will refresh your heart as a sweet rain refreshes the thirsty earth. My dear child, let your confidence in God be unshaken. There is nothing he will not do for those he loves. He conducts us by grief to unmingled happiness. Do you recollect, my dear Mary, all the grief which you felt when, after our painful walk, I fell down with fatigue in the middle of the road? Well, this accident was the means which the Lord made use of to procure for us the sweet rest which we have enjoyed for three years with these good people.

Without this sickness we should either not have come before their door, or they would not have been touched with so much compassion. All the pleasures which we have here tasted, all the good which we have been enabled to do, all the happy days which we have here spent, are so many benefits which resulted from this sickness.

" It is thus, my dear Mary, that in the troubles of this life we can find proofs of the divine goodness. If the liberal hand of the Lord has scattered with flowers mountains and valleys, forests and the banks of rivers, and even muddy marshes, to give us everywhere the opportunity of admiring his tenderness and goodness, he has also imprinted on all the events of our life evident traces of his great wisdom, and of his compassionate love for men, in order that an attentive mind may learn by them to love and adore Him. Every one can observe them in his own life, if he is capable of a little attention. Never have we had more to suffer than when you were accused of theft, when you were put in chains and likely to be condemned to death, when we were together weeping and lamenting in prison.

" Well, this evil trial has been a source of good to us. Yes, those blessings are visible now!

When the young Countess distinguished you from the other young girls, did you the honour to admit you to her company, made you a present of a beautiful gown, and wished you to be always near her, no doubt you thought yourself very happy. But it was to be feared that those honours, those luxuries, and those vanities would render you vain, trifling, fond of the things of this world, and apt to forget God. The Lord then consulted our interest only when he changed our situation and made us unhappy. In misery, in poverty, in prison, we have lived near to him; he has conducted us far from the dissipations of a corrupt world into this rude country, where he has prepared for you a better dwelling. You are like a flower which embellishes the most secret solitude, where it has nothing to fear from the hand of man. It is he, it is this good and faithful God, who wishes to give a still more happy turn to the misfortunes which you have suffered.

"Yes, I firmly believe he has answered my prayer—yes, he will one day show the world your innocence. When this time shall come I may be no more; but, convinced as I am of your innocence, I need not to see you justified in order to die in tranquillity. Yes, Mary, the pain which you have suffered will yet be the means of leading you to joy and happiness on earth, though this kind of happiness is the least, and to see that God's great design in afflicting us was to prepare us for heaven, to which we can arrive only through suffering and tribulation. Thus in misfortune let not care trouble your soul; believe that God's tenderness watches over you, that his care will be sufficient for you, and in whatever place he chooses to conduct you to, in whatever painful situation you may be placed, say, ' It is the place —the most advantageous situation for me, notwithstanding all that I suffer.' Believe that it is exactly the position in which to perfect your virtue, and for you to do the will of your Saviour who died for you."

So much exertion caused the old man to feel faint for a time; but after a few hours he continued his advice. " A gardener, my dear Mary," he said, " assigns to each plant the spot he thinks will be the most proper to make it prosper. In the same manner God assigns to every believer that station in life which suits him best, and in which he will make the greatest progress in holiness. And thus, my dear Mary, as he has until now turned to your advantage all your misfortunes, he will also bless to you my last sickness and death. I cannot pronounce the word death without causing you to shed a torrent of tears. But do not think that death is so terrible. Let us once speak as we formerly did in our garden at Terborg. You know what happens at the beginning of spring: small and weak plants sprout out together from narrow and moist beds; it is not then supposed that they will produce beautiful flowers or delicious fruits, and indeed they will bear neither fruits nor flowers if they remain crowded in this narrow space; they will want room; and the gardener who placed them there does not wish them to remain there and die. He designs to transplant them into an open space, where they may be revived by the pure air, and be exposed under the azure of a beautiful sky to the golden rays of the sun. At last, watered by rain and dew, they put forth leaves, and shine in all their beauty. It was always a pleasure to you when I transplanted these young shoots, for you used to say they crowded one another in the beds. You were only satisfied when they were in an open space. ' Now,' you would say, ' they will grow finely—I think that I see them do so already.'

"My dear daughter, we are poor weak plants; the earth which we inhabit is a narrow bed; this is not our abode—here we are but miserable vegetables; but we are destined to become something greater and more perfect. That is the reason why God transplants us into large and beautiful gardens—in a word, to heaven.

"Cease your weeping, my dear child. See how much better I bear my prospect of departure. Oh, how I rejoice to go so soon to my Saviour! What a happiness to be delivered from this body which has done so much evil in the world, and to be with Christ for ever! Dear Mary, do you remember the great pleasure we took in our garden on a beautiful spring morning? Heaven is compared to the most beautiful of all gardens, where an eternal spring for ever reigns. It is for this delightful country I am going to set out. Oh! continue to serve God, and we shall be there at last united. Here we have been together only to suffer tribulations without number—we have been separated only to weep and lament. But there we shall remain together in the midst of joy and beatitude, without the fear of separation. Mary, live always close to God, and if you are reserved for a happy life here below, let not these passing joys make you forget the joys of eternity. Then your mother and I shall meet our daughter in heaven. Do not then weep, my dear child, but rather rejoice in the prospect of the future."

It was thus that this good father attempted to console his daughter, who was soon to be left alone on the earth. It was thus that he endeavoured, by his advice, to fortify her against the corruptions of the world. Every word was a good seed which fell on well-prepared ground. " I have caused you much grief and many tears, my dear child," he said at length; " but they are salutary tears. Seeds sown among tears take root more easily, and thrive much better than when no deep emotion is stirred; they are like grain which when sown is watered by the soft showers of spring."

CHAPTER XII

THE DEATH OF JACOB

When Mary found that her father could not survive much longer, she went to Erlenbrunn, the parish to which Pine Farm belonged, and informed the pastor of the illness of her father. Being an exemplary and pious man he paid Jacob a number of visits, and had some edifying conversations with him, and never failed to say a few words of comfort and encouragement to Mary. One afternoon when he paid his visit, he found the old man very much weaker. Jacob requested Mary to leave the room for a moment, in order that he might have a few minutes' conversation with the pastor alone. He soon called her in again and said, "My dear Mary, I have now settled all my worldly affairs, and our good pastor has consented to administer the last sacrament to me to-morrow morning."

Mary was much distressed, and had great difficulty in restraining her tears, for she saw that the fatal moment was not far off. But she immediately recomposed herself, and said: "You are right, my dear Father! What better can we do when in pain and trouble than have recourse to God?"

Jacob spent the remainder of the day and evening in silent prayer. He was in a state of holy meditation, and spoke but little. Next day he received the holy communion at the hands of the pastor with indescribable joy. Faith, love, and the hope of eternal life caused his venerable countenance to become radiant with celestial happiness, while tears of transcendent bliss ran down his cheeks. Mary, on her knees beside his bed, trembled, wept, and prayed. The farmer, his wife, and all their household contemplated this solemn edifying scene with deep emotions. Their hands were clasped, and almost every eye was wet with tears.

"Now," said Mary afterwards, "I feel as though my heart had been relieved of a burden, and I am greatly consoled. It is indeed true that the religion of Jesus Christ affords us not only in life, but at the hour of death, the most heavenly consolation."

Meanwhile Jacob felt his end rapidly approaching. The farmer and his wife, who honoured and cherished him as their best friend, and blessed the day that brought him into their house, did everything they could think of to comfort and solace his last hours. Ten times a day would they come—now one and now the other—to inquire how he was; and each time Mary would inquire with mingled grief and affection in her voice: "Don't you think that he may yet recover?"

Once the farmer's wife gave her for answer, "Oh! my child, I certainly do not think that he can hold out longer than the coming of the leaves on the trees."

From that time Mary continually sat at her little window, and, trembling, watched the budding of the flowers in her garden. Hitherto the return of spring had always filled her with joy; but now the leaves of the gooseberry bushes and the budding of the trees filled her with sadness. The joyous chirping of the chaffinch overwhelmed her with terror; and when she saw the flowers of the snowdrop and the primrose she was deeply affected.

"Ah!" she exclaimed, "everything is renewed —everything in nature smiles! Must my dear father be without hope and die?" And then checking herself, she raised her eyes to heaven, and said, "No, not without hope! no, no! Jesus has said he shall not die—'he that believeth in me shall not die'. He only puts off this earthly tabernacle, this house of clay, in order that he may enjoy a new and better life in heaven above."

It gave the old man great pleasure to hear Mary read to him, she did it in so sweet and clear a voice. During the latter part of his illness he liked to hear nothing better than the last words of Jesus, and his last prayer. Once during the night his daughter was sitting beside his bed; the beams of the moon shone so brightly into the room that the light of the taper was scarcely visible.

"Mary," said the invalid, "read me once more that beautiful prayer of our Saviour."

Opening her father's Bible she read as he desired.

"Now," said he, "give me the book, and hold the light a little nearer to me." Mary gave him the book, and placed the candle so that it lighted the page.

"Now," said he, "this will be the last prayer that I shall make for you." He marked the passage with his finger, and prayed in a trembling voice: "O Father, I have not long to remain in this world, but this, my child, will be left here for a little while. I am coming—I dare to hope—

to thee, Father! But before I go, holy and almighty God, I venture to ask thee once more to
preserve my child from sin, for thy name's sake.
While I have been on earth, I have endeavoured
in thy name to preserve her from the contamina-
tion of the world. But, O Lord, I am now coming
to thee. I do not ask thee to take her to thee, but
only to preserve her from harm. Let thy holy
truth support her. Thy word is truth. Grant, O
heavenly Father, that the child which thou hast
given me may be at last admitted to the place
where I hope to go, through Jesus my Saviour.
Amen."

Mary, who stood beside his bed bathed in
tears, repeated as well as her sobs would allow
her, "Amen."

"Yes," he continued, "my dear daughter,
there we shall see Jesus in his kingdom, which
he had from the beginning of the world, and
there we shall once more meet each other."

He laid himself down on his pillow to rest a
little. He continued to hold the Bible in his
hand. It was one he had bought since he left
Terborg, with the first money saved from his
scanty earnings.

"Dear Mary," he said some moments afterwards, "I thank you again most sincerely for all the affection and tenderness which you have shown me since my illness commenced, and which will be the last I shall have need of here. You have well and faithfully observed the fifth commandment. Bear in mind the promise given to those who honour and obey their parents. I implicitly believe, my dear child, that it will be fulfilled to you, though I am obliged to leave you poor and helpless. I can give you nothing but my blessing and this book. Be always pious and good, and this blessing will not be without effect. The blessing of a father, with confidence in the Lord, is better for a virtuous child than the richest inheritance. Take this Bible, and let it be a remembrance of your father. It cost me, it is true, but a few shillings, but let it be faithfully read, the precepts therein contained put in practice, and then I shall have left you the richest treasure. If I had left you as many pieces of gold as the spring produces leaves and flowers, with all that money you could not buy anything better; for this book contains the word of God. Read it every morning—no matter what work you have to do, time should always be found for that— read at least one passage—preserve it and meditate upon it in your heart during the day. If you discover any obscurity, pray for the Holy Spirit to enlighten you, as I have always done, and with infinite profit. All that is most essential in the book may be understood by everybody. Hold fast to that, follow it faithfully, and it will not fail to draw upon you the blessing of Heaven. This passage alone, ' Consider the lilies of the field ', has afforded me more lessons of wisdom than all the books which I read in my youth; and besides that, it has been the source to me of a thousand pleasures. My innumerable sorrows would have filled me with unceasing anxiety—I should have been endlessly discouraged and dejected—if this passage had not afforded me the foundation for a serene and happy spirit."

About three o'clock in the morning Jacob faintly said, " I feel very ill—open the window a little."

Mary opened it; the moon had disappeared, but the sky covered with stars presented a magnificent spectacle. " See how beautiful the sky appears!" said the sick man. " What are the flowers of earth when compared with those stars, whose beauty suffers no diminution. It is there I am now going. Oh, what joy! I am going to my Lord and Saviour! Keep close to Him, my dear child, and soon we shall meet again!"

As he uttered these words he fell upon his bed and died the death of a Christian.

Mary thought he had only fainted, for she had never seen anyone die, and did not think he was so near his end; nevertheless in her fright she awoke all the family; they ran to the old man's bed-side, and then she heard them declare he was dead. She embraced his cold remains, kissed his pale face, and wept bitterly.

" Oh, my father—my good father," cried she, " how shall I now repay you for all the goodness you have shown to me? Alas! I cannot —I can only thank you for all the words, for all the good advice that I have received from that mouth, those lips, now sealed in death. It is with gratitude that I kiss your hand, now cold and stiff.—that hand which bestowed on me so many benefits, which laboured so much for my good, and which in my childhood chastised me with so much loving-kindness. I now see for the first time how well meant it was, and how good it was for me. Oh, receive my thanks —receive my heartfelt thanks for all your goodness, and forgive me if I have grieved you by my

childish thoughtlessness! Oh, God, repay him
for all his love to me! Oh, when my time comes,
' let me die the death of the righteous ', as this
man, my father, has done! How little—how very
little there is in this life on earth! How good it
is that there is a heaven, and an everlasting life!
that is now my only consolation."

The scene was heartrending. At last the
farmer's wife, after entreating Mary for some
time, prevailed upon her to lie down. Nothing
would induce her during the following day to
leave the body of her father. She read, wept,
and prayed alternately the night through. Before the coffin lid was nailed down, Mary took
one more look at her father. "Alas!" said she,
" it is the last time that I shall ever behold that
beloved face. How beautiful it was when you
smiled, and it shone with the glory into which
you were going to enter! Farewell—farewell,
my father!" she cried, sobbing aloud; " may
your mortal remains rest peaceably in the bosom
of the earth, now while the angels of the Lord
are, as I hope, bearing your soul to eternal rest."

She gathered rosemary, primroses as yellow
as gold, and violets of a deep blue. She made
a bouquet of them, and placed them on the

bosom of her father, who during his life had sown and cultivated so many flowers. " May these flowers, the first-fruits of the spring," said she, " be an image of your future resurrection; and this rosemary, always green, the symbol of the pious recollection that will be for ever engraven on my heart."

When they began to nail down the coffin lid, every stroke of the hammer caused her so much emotion that she almost fainted. The farmer's wife led her into the next room, and begged her to lie on the bed to recover herself.

Mary attended the funeral of her father in a deep mourning dress lent to her for the occasion by a sympathetic maiden of the village. She followed close to the body of her father. Her face was as pale as death, and every one pitied the poor forsaken orphan, who now had neither father nor mother.

As Mary's father was a stranger in the district, they dug a grave for him in the corner of the cemetery against the wall. Beside this wall were two large pine-trees which shaded the tomb. The pastor preached a touching sermon from the text: " Except a corn of wheat fall into the ground and die, it abideth alone; but if it die, it bringeth forth much fruit," John xii, 24. He spoke of Jacob's patience, and of the resignation with which he had borne all the misfortunes that had fallen to his lot, and the good example he had set to those who knew him. He said a few words of consolation to the orphan, who was overwhelmed with grief. He thanked, in the name of the deceased, the farmer and his wife, who had so well proved to Mary and her father the kindness of their hearts. In short, he begged them to be father and mother to Mary, who had no longer any parents.

Whenever Mary attended divine service she never failed to visit the tomb. She went also every Sunday evening, when the opportunity offered, to visit the tomb of her father, and to weep over his cherished remains. " Nowhere," would she say, " have I prayed with so much fervour as here at my father's grave. Here the whole world is nothing to me. I feel that we belong to a better world. My heart sighs for that country, because I daily feel the evil of the one in which I now am." She never left the grave without having made good resolutions to despise the pleasures of the world, and to live only to her God.

CHAPTER XIII

MARY STILL SOWING IN TEARS

From the time of her father's death Mary was constantly sad. The flowers had in her eyes lost all their beauty; and the pines near the farm looked as though they were clothed in black. Time, it is true, moderated her grief, but soon she had new trials to undergo.

Great changes had taken place at Pine Farm since the death of her father. The farmer had given up the farm to his only son, a man of good temper and amiable disposition, but unhappy in the choice of his wife, whom he had married a short time before. She was called handsome, and was possessed of considerable property. But she was vain of her beauty, and cared for nothing but money. Pride and avarice had by degrees imprinted on her features an expression of harshness so striking, that with all her comeliness her looks were repulsive. She had no religion in her heart, and not having the wholesome restraints of the gospel, if she knew that anything would give the old people pleasure, she did just the contrary. Even when she gave them their food, which was their due according to the contract they had made between them, which was that they should be supported for the remainder of their days, it was always with a bad grace and with sordid parsimony. She sought continually to mortify them, and made their lives miserable to the last degree. The poor old couple retired into the little back chamber, and seldom appeared in the front room.

The young husband, too, was no happier than his parents; the wicked woman overwhelmed him with the grossest abuse, and cast into his teeth a hundred times a day the money she had brought him. If he would not spend the day in quarrelling and disputing, he was obliged to suffer in silence. She would never quietly allow him to visit his parents, for fear, as she said, he would give them something secretly. In the evening, after he had finished his work, he scarcely dared to go near them. He found them almost always seated side by side in the utmost sadness. He would take a seat by them, and complain of his hard lot.

"Well, well," replied the old man, "such is the way of the world. Your mother allowed herself to be dazzled by the glitter of her gold; you were taken by her rosy cheeks; I yielded too easily to your wishes, and thus we are all punished. We should have thought of the good advice of old Jacob; he was an experienced man, and never approved of this match when it was talked of during his life. I still remember every word he said on the subject, and I have thought of it more than a thousand times. Do you remember," he said, turning to his wife, "having one day said, 'But ten thousand florins is worth having! It is a beautiful sum of money!'"

The old woman said she remembered.

"And well do I recollect Jacob's answer," continued the old farmer. "'Do not call it a beautiful sum,' he said. 'The flowers you see in your garden are a thousand times more beautiful. Perhaps you meant to say it is a large and heavy sum. I will acknowledge that. He must have good shoulders who can bear it without being bowed down to the earth, and without becoming a poor wretch, unable to raise his head to heaven. Why then wish for so much money? You have never wanted for anything; so far from it, you have always had more than sufficient. Believe me, to have too much money is no blessing; it is as bad as to have too little. Rain is useful and necessary; but when too much falls there is great danger of its destroying the most healthy plants of the garden.'

"These are exactly the words of the old friend we have lost; I fancy I can still hear him. And you, my son, once said to him, 'She is a charming girl, and as beautiful and fresh as a rose.' 'Flowers,' answered the wise old man, 'have not beauty only—they are useful and pretty at the same time. They make us many rich presents; the bee extracts from them pure wax and delicious honey. Without piety, a beautiful exterior is but a rose upon paper, a miserable trifle, without life and without perfume, which produces neither wax nor honey.' Such were the reflections which Jacob frankly made before us. We would not listen to him—now we know how to appreciate his advice. That which appeared to us then so great a happiness is now to us the height of misfortune. God give us the grace to bear our misfortunes with patience."

Thus they used frequently to talk together.

As to poor Mary she also had much to suffer.

The old people were obliged to occupy the back room. She therefore gave up her place to them. The young wife had two rooms empty, but through unkindness she gave Mary the most miserable apartment in the house, ill-treated her in every possible way, and loaded her with abuse. There was nothing but fault-finding from morning till night. Mary, according to her, did not work enough, and did not know how to do anything as it ought to be done. It was very plainly to be seen by the poor orphan that she was despised, and a trouble to the house. The old man and his wife were not in a situation to offer her any consolation; they had enough to do with their own griefs. She thought often of going away, but where to go she knew not. She asked the pastor's advice.

"My dear Mary," said the good man, "to remain any longer at the Pine Farm is a thing impossible. Your father gave you an excellent education, and had you trained in everything that is necessary for the management of a tradesman's family. But at Pine Farm they put more hard work upon you than a rough country girl, used to the toil of a farm, could do. The labour they require of you is beyond your strength, and is not suited to your training or condition. However, I would not advise you to leave immediately, and to go alone into the wide world on the chance of finding a situation that would be more agreeable to you. The best advice I can give you is, to remain where you are for the present; to work as much as you can, and to wait patiently until the Lord shall deliver you from the state of oppression under which you sigh. The Saviour who raised you to another condition is still able to sustain you. I will endeavour to get you a place in an honest and Christian family. Pray unceasingly; have confidence in God; bear your trials with patience, and God will arrange all things for your good."

Mary thanked him, and promised to follow his good advice.

In all her troubles there was one spot where Mary could always find comfort and solace; it was the grave of her father. There she seemed to be brought nearer to him; all his kindly advice and wise instruction seemed to come back to her as she lingered about where his ashes had been laid. She had planted a rose-tree there. "Alas!" she mourned, as she planted the shrub, "if I could remain here always, I would water you with my tears, and you would soon be covered with flowers and leaves.

The rose-tree was already covered with leaves, and the tender buds began to open their crimson cups. " My father was right," said Mary, " when he compared human life to a rose-tree. Sometimes it is quite withered and bare; it offers to the eye nothing but thorns. But wait a little, and the season will return when it will be clothed anew with foliage, and adorned with the most beautiful flowers. This is now for me the time of thorns, but God forbid that I should be cast down by it. I believe your word, best of fathers. Perhaps I may see verified in my life your maxim —' Patience produces roses. ' "

CHAPTER XIV

THE LAST AND HEAVIEST TRIAL

In the midst of all Mary's troubles, the 25th of July arrived, the anniversary of her father's birthday. Until then it had always been to her a day of joy, but this time she hailed with tears the rising of the sun, whose gilded rays illumined her chamber. In former days she had always prepared for this day something which she knew would give her father pleasure; but now he was gone. The country people in the neighbourhood were in the habit of ornamenting with flowers the graves of their dearest friends, particularly at the time of such anniversaries. They had often entreated Mary to give them flowers, and she always took pleasure in gratifying their wishes. She now thought of decorating her father's tomb in the same manner. The beautiful though ill-fated basket, which had been the first cause of her unhappiness, was standing before her on the cupboard.

Mary took it and filled it with flowers of all

colours and with fresh leaves, carried it to Erlenbrunn an hour before divine service, and de-
posited it on her father's grave. Her tears fell
upon the flowers, and glittered like dew upon the
fresh leaves. " Oh! the best and dearest of
fathers," she said, " you strewed for me the path
of life with flowers. If I cannot do as much for
you, I will at least ornament your grave with
them." Mary left the basket on the tomb; she
had no fear that any one would dare to steal
either the basket or the flowers. At a little distance the country people contemplated this offering with joy mingled with pity, blessed in their
hearts Jacob's pious daughter, and prayed for her
prosperity.

The following day, as the people of the farm
were making hay in a large meadow situated
beyond the forest, a piece of fine linen, which
was spread out to bleach on the grass near a
rivulet a few steps from the house, suddenly
disappeared. The young farmer's wife did not
miss it until the evening. Being very suspicious,
as all misers are, she immediately blamed Mary.
Honest Jacob had made no secret of the unfortunate story of the ring, but had confided every
circumstance connected with it to the old farmer

and his wife. Their son, who had heard it, imprudently related it to his wife. In the evening, when Mary, a rake on her shoulder and an earthen pitcher in her hand, entered the house with the servants, the wicked woman came out of the kitchen, and met her with a torrent of abuse, and ordered her to produce the linen immediately.

The poor girl answered with the greatest gentleness that it was impossible she could have taken the linen, as she had spent the whole day in the hayfield with the other work-people, adding that a stranger might easily have taken advantage of a moment when there was no one in the kitchen to commit the theft. This conjecture was indeed the truth. The farmer's wife, however, would not listen to reason, but cried out in a paroxysm of rage. " You thief! Do you think I don't know of the theft of the ring, and what difficulty you had to escape the hands of the executioner? Get out of the house this instant. There is no room under my roof for such as you!"

" It is too late," said the husband, " to send her away to-night. The sun has already set. Let her sup with us, as she has worked hard all day in the greatest heat, and must be hungry and tired. In the morning she can go away if you still wish it."

" Not even an hour," said the wicked woman,
" shall she stay in my house. And you had better
hold your tongue, or I will stop your mouth with
a burning stick from the fire."

The poor man saw that anything he could say
would only serve to irritate her still more, and
was therefore silent. Mary made no answer to
the accusations of the farmer's wife. She wrapped
up the little she possessed in a clean napkin, quite
large enough to contain all, put the little bundle
under her arm, thanked the inhabitants of the
Pine Farm for the services they had done her,
protested once more her innocence, and asked
permission to take leave of the old people who
had been her benefactors. " You may do that,"
said the woman, with a disdainful smile; " and
if you would take them with you it would give
me great pleasure. It is evident that death is in
no hurry to rid me of them."

The good old people had heard the distur-
bance, and both wept for Mary's sake. They
consoled her as well as they could, and gave her
what money they had to assist her on her way.
" Go, good girl," they said to her, " and may
God be with you. The blessing of your father is
a precious treasure for you, and one of these days

will bring you happiness. Remember us kindly in your prosperity, for things will yet go well with you."

Mary set out towards the close of the day with her little bundle under her arm, and began to climb up the mountain, following a narrow road in the woods. She wished to visit once more her father's grave. When she came out of the forest the village clock struck seven, and before she arrived at the graveyard it was nearly dark; but she was not afraid to pass the night in the midst of the graves. She went to her father's tomb, and her tears fell in torrents.

The full moon shone through the dark foliage of the two pines, and illumined, with a silver light, the roses on the grave, and the BASKET OF FLOWERS. A gentle breeze blew with a soft murmur among the branches of the pine-trees, and agitated also the trembling leaves of the rose-tree planted on the tomb.

" My dear father," said Mary, " why are you not still here to hear my complaints? But it is better, and it is a blessing for which I thank God, that you do not live to witness this affliction. You are now happy, and inaccessible to grief. Oh! why am I not with you? Alas! never was

I so much to be pitied as now. When the moon illumined my prison through the iron bars, you were then alive. Oh, my dear father! now it illumines your grave. When we were driven from the country that we loved so much, you at least were still with me, and I had in you a good father, a protector, and faithful friend. Now I have no one. Poor, forsaken, suspected of crime, a stranger—I am alone in the world, and know not where to lay my head. A little corner remained to me on this earth—one little corner—and behold I am driven from it. My last consolation was to come from time to time and weep on your grave; of this comfort also I am deprived."

At these words she began again to weep.

"Oh, gracious God!" she cried, as she sank upon her knees, "kind Father in heaven, deign to look down upon a poor forsaken orphan, who weeps upon the grave of her earthly father, and have pity upon me. When our need is greatest, thy need is ever nearest. My grief could not be greater, and my heart is ready almost to break. Oh! show me that thy arm is not shortened—that thou art still as mighty as ever to save. Forsake me not, O Lord, for I have no one to help me but thou. Take me to thyself in heaven, where my good parents are, or send a little drop of comfort to cheer my fainting heart! When the flowers are weak and drooping after the glowing heat of the day, thou sendest the refreshing dew to revive them in the cool moonlight. Oh, have pity—have pity on me!"

"Alas!" she exclaimed, when she had become a little calmer, "what shall I do? and where shall I go? I dare not at this hour approach any house to ask for shelter. Were I to say I had been turned out-of-doors it is hardly likely that any one would consent to receive me."

She looked round her. Against the church-yard wall, and near her father's grave, was a gravestone, very old and covered with moss. As the inscription on it had been long since effaced, and it was in the way, it had been put on one side, and used as a seat.

"I will sit down on this stone," she said, "and pass the night near the tomb of my father. It may be the last time I shall ever be here. Perhaps I shall never again see this grave, which is so dear to me. In the morning, before the break of day, I will go forth once more into the wide world, trusting in the guidance of Almighty God to lead me whither he would have me go."

CHAPTER XV

HELP COMES FROM HEAVEN

Mary sat down on the stone near the wall, and under the thick foliage of a pine, which covered her with its dark branches. She hid her face in her handkerchief, all bathed in tears. Her soul was troubled, and she breathed from the bottom of her heart prayers so fervent that language would fail to express them.

"Oh, heavenly Father," she sobbed, "hast thou no angel to show me the way wherein I should go?"

Scarcely had she finished when she heard a sweet voice calling her familiarly by her name, "Mary, Mary." She looked up and trembled with fear. Before her, in the beautiful moonlight, stood a fair and lovely form, with eyes beaming with celestial light, cheeks of the tenderest pink, like opening peach-blossoms, head and shoulders enveloped in a profusion of rich golden curls, and clothed in a long flowing robe of the purest white. Mary sank, frightened and trembling, on her knees, and cried, "Has God really sent an angel from heaven to help me?"

"Dear Mary," said this being, in the most kindly manner, "be not alarmed. I am not an angel from heaven, I am only a mortal like yourself; but I come all the same to help you. God has heard your fervent prayers. Look at me; is it possible you do not know me?"

With an exclamation of surprise Mary cried, "Is it you—the Countess Amelia? Oh, how did you get here—here, in so frightful a place, at this hour of night, so far from your home?"

The young Countess raised Mary gently from the ground, pressed her to her heart, and kissed her tenderly.

"Dear Mary," she said, "we have done you a great injustice. You have been ill rewarded for the pleasure you once gave me by the present of the basket of flowers. But at last your innocence has been established. Oh, can you forgive us? Can you forgive my parents and me? Come, we are ready to make reparation, as far as it lies in our power, for all the wrongs that you have suffered. Forgive us, dear Mary."

"Do not speak so, gracious lady," said Mary weeping. "Considering all the circumstances,

you were very forbearing towards me. I have
never felt the least resentment towards you. I
only thought with gratitude of your kindness.
My only sorrow was that you and your dear
parents should regard me as an ungrateful and
wicked girl. My most ardent desire was that you
might one day be convinced of my innocence,
and this prayer God has now granted. Thanks
be to Him!"

The Countess pressed Mary to her heart, and
bathed her face in tears. Then she looked down
at the grave at her feet, and clasping her hands,
exclaimed in accents of grief, " Oh, good and
noble man, whose remains here repose in the
bosom of the earth—thou whom I learned to love
from my most tender infancy, whose affectionate
counsels I have so often received, and to whose
fervent prayers I have so often listened,—why
cannot I see thy face to ask thy pardon for all the
injury we so unjustly did thee? Ah! if we had
taken more precautions, if we had placed more
confidence in an old servant, who had always
shown the most unimpeachable probity and
fidelity, thy remains would not now, perhaps, be
lying here; thou hadst still been living with us.
Oh, that I could have heard you forgive us! But

as that cannot be, behold, here on thy grave, and in the name of my parents, I solemnly vow that the atonement we can no longer make to thee shall be made in double measure to thy daughter. Would that we could have been sure of his forgiveness!" exclaimed Amelia in conclusion.

"Ah! gracious lady," said Mary, "my father was very far from feeling the least resentment towards the family he had served so long. He included you in his prayers every evening and morning, as he was accustomed to do while we lived in Terborg. He blessed you all at the hour of his death. 'Mary,' he said, a little while before he died, 'I feel perfectly confident that those whom we served will one day recognize your innocence, and will recall you from exile. Assure, then, the noble Count, the kind-hearted Countess, and the dear angel Amelia, whom I so often carried in my arms when she was a child, that my heart was full of the deepest respect, of love, and gratitude towards them till my last breath.' Be assured, my dear lady, those were his last words."

"Come, Mary," said she, "come and sit down here beside me on this stone. I cannot leave your father's grave till I have told you how God has brought to light your innocence.

CHAPTER XVI

THE HAND OF PROVIDENCE

" God is surely with you, dear Mary," said the young Countess, after they had seated themselves upon the tomb. " He has taken you under his protection. It is he who has marvellously conducted me here to assist you. There is nothing but what is simple and natural in the recital which I shall give you. You will, however, see in it a chain of truly providential circumstances.

" From the time that your innocence was made known to us," she continued, " I had no more happiness. You and your father were always present to my mind. Believe me, dear Mary, I have shed many tears on your account. My parents sought for you everywhere, but without being able to obtain any trace of you. Three days ago I came with my father and mother to the hunting lodge belonging to the Prince which is situated in the forest, not far from the village. It has not been inhabited for twenty years, except by a forester who acts as caretaker. My father, as you know, is the keeper of the royal forests, and he had a dispute relating to a question of boundary to settle. This it was which brought him hither. He spent the whole of to-day in the forest, in company with two strange gentlemen who are concerned in the affair. These noblemen came accompanied by their wives and a young lady, the daughter of one of them, and Mother was obliged to devote the evening to their entertainment. It had been extremely warm during the day, and the evening was so cool and pleasant, the setting sun offered so beautiful a spectacle, the mountains covered with forests of pines, and interspersed with picturesque rocks, were so novel a spectacle, and afforded me a pleasure so lively, that I begged Mother's permission to take a short walk. The gamekeeper's daughter accompanied me.

"As we passed through the village we found the gate of the churchyard open. The tombstones were gilded by the rays of the setting sun. I have ever since my childhood taken a deep pleasure in reading inscriptions and epitaphs: I am moved when one tells of a young man or woman carried off in the bloom of youth; I

experience a melancholy pleasure if I find that it
records the death of a man or woman who had
reached an exceptionally advanced age.   Even
the verses, although the sentiments which dictate
them are often better than the language in which
they are clothed, frequently suggest to me good
thoughts and useful resolutions, which I store
up in my memory.

"We went, therefore, into the churchyard.
After I had read a great number of the inscriptions, the gamekeeper's daughter said to me,
'I want to show you something very beautiful;
it is the grave of an old man. You will find there
neither tombstone nor epitaph, but it has been
most tastefully adorned with flowers by his
daughter, who loved him most tenderly. Do you
see, through the thick foliage of these pines, a
beautiful rose-tree, and a pretty basket of flowers
placed on the grave?'

"I went to the spot, and stood petrified with
amazement. At the first glance I recognized the
basket which had been in my mind's eye a thousand times since you left Terborg. I drew near to
look at it, and if I had had any doubts, the initials
of my name and the arms of my family would
have removed them. I questioned my companion

about your history, and that of your father. She
told me that you had been residing at Pine Farm,
and related to me some particulars of the last
sickness and death of your father, and the grief
which it had caused you. I hastened to see the
pastor, whom I found a very worthy man. He
confirmed all that I had before heard, and praised
you very, very much. I wished then to go to
Pine Farm, but while I was talking with the
clergyman time had flown so rapidly that it was
already quite dark.

"'What is to be done?' said I; 'it is now too
late to go to the farm, and to-morrow at daybreak we leave the neighbourhood.'

"Then the pastor sent for the schoolmaster,
and asked him to go and bring you without delay
to the parsonage.

"'Do you mean the poor stranger, Mary?'
asked the schoolmaster when the clergyman had
told him what he wished him to do. 'There is
no need to go so far as the farm to fetch her.
She went a little while ago to her father's grave,
and there she is weeping and lamenting. Alas!
poor child,' said he, 'I fear she will go out of her
mind through grief. I saw her from an opening
in the steeple when I went to wind up the clock.'

"The pastor wished to accompany me to your father's grave; but I begged him to allow me to go alone, so that I might speak to you freely without witnesses, and yielding to my importunities, he went to tell my parents where I was, lest they should be anxious, and to prepare them for your arrival. This will account, my dear Mary, for my sudden and somewhat strange appearance. Thus, through the interposition of divine providence, this basket of flowers has reunited us at your father's grave."

"Yes," said Mary, clasping her hands, and raising her grateful eyes to heaven, "God has done it all. He has had pity on my tears, and on the extremity to which I was reduced. Oh, what goodness—what loving-kindness he has shown towards me!"

"I have still one more circumstance to tell you, my dear Mary," answered the Countess, interrupting her; "one feature of this history appears to me singularly touching and inspires me with the greatest awe for the justice of God, who often directs our lot unknown to ourselves. Juliette, the greatest enemy you have upon earth, had but one thought, one desire, which was to banish you from my heart, and to confirm herself in your place. It was with this view that she invented the wicked falsehood she told, and her atrocious plot appeared to her to have succeeded to perfection. But it was this falsehood that in the end caused her to lose her place, and our confidence, and that rendered you more dear than ever to our hearts. She endeavoured to estrange you for ever from me. Your banishment was a continual subject of triumph to her. In the excess of her malignant joy she went and threw at your feet this basket with an insulting laugh; and it was this event which—she little thought it then —was destined afterwards to reunite us for ever. For was it not by means of the basket that I discovered you here? It is true that if we love God we have nothing to fear from those who would do us evil, for God knows how to turn to our advantage all the ill that wicked people can do us; and thus our most cruel enemies, in all that they attempt against us, can do nothing in reality but contribute to our happiness. That good comes out of evil is a divine truth that nothing can gainsay.

"But now that I have told you all this," continued the young Countess after a pause, "you must tell me, my dear Mary, the reason for your coming so late to your father's grave, and why you were crying so bitterly."

Mary related the circumstances that led to her being driven from the farm, which caused the Countess fresh astonishment and grief.

"But never mind!" said Amelia, "your being sent away led to our meeting all the quicker." Then, after a pause, she added, "It was by God's will that I arrived here just at the time when you were plunged in deepest distress, when you were imploring his assistance in an accent so sorrowful, and when scalding tears were running down your cheeks. You again see in this a surprising proof of the truth that 'God knows how to turn to our advantage the ill our enemies design to do us'. The farmer's wicked wife, who drove you from her house, thought she would make you unhappy; but she has conducted you to my arms, and those of my parents, who, as well as myself, are desirous of making you happy. But it is time for us to be going," Amelia continued: "my parents will be waiting for me. Come, dear Mary, I will never leave you again, and to-morrow you must return with us to Terborg."

Mary could not help feeling a pang of grief at the thought that she might never again have the opportunity to look upon her father's grave, and it was with difficulty that she dragged herself away from the silent churchyard.

Amelia at length took her gently by the arm, and said kindly, "Come! come away, my dear Mary, and bring with you the basket of flowers, so that you may always have a memento of your dear father. Instead of the basket with which your devoted love adorned his tomb, we will have a more lasting monument erected. That, I am sure, will please you. Come, you must be impatient to hear the history of the ring, which I will relate to you as we go along."

Amelia put her arm through Mary's, and the two walked together towards the old castle, being lighted on their way by the soft light of the moon.

CHAPTER XVII

HOW MARY'S INNOCENCE WAS DISCOVERED

A long avenue of tall old linden-trees led to the castle. After Amelia and Mary had walked along for some time in silence, stirred by varied emotions, the young Countess said, "I must now tell you how the ring was found.

"We left the capital this year earlier than usual, as business required my father's presence at Terborg. We arrived there amid beautiful spring weather in the early days of March. We had not been there many days, however, before the weather changed. One night in particular we had a tremendous storm. You will remember the enormous pear-tree we had in our garden in Terborg. It was already very old, and bore scarcely any fruit. The wind, which that night blew with great violence, damaged and caused it to lean over so much that it threatened every moment to fall. My father therefore ordered it to be cut down. All the servants were obliged to assist, in order that it might be felled with such care as not to injure the other trees in its fall.

My father and mother, we children, and indeed all the people in the castle had come into the garden to see the last of the old tree.

"When the tree had come down with a great crash my two little brothers ran to seize a nest of magpies which was in the tree, and which had been for a long time an object of great curiosity to them. They now examined it with great attention. 'Look, brother,' said Augustus, 'what is that shining so brightly amongst the mass of twigs?' 'It sparkles like,' said Albert, 'gold and precious stones.'

"Juliette, always inquisitive, ran forward to look. Then, with a shrill cry, she exclaimed, 'It is the ring!' and became as pale as death.

"The boys released the ring from twigs with which it had been interwoven, and carried it immediately, in great glee, to my mother.

"'Yes, it is the ring,' said my mother. 'Oh, good, honest Jacob! Oh, poor Mary! what injustice we have done you! I am very glad to find the ring again; but I should be much more so if I could find Jacob and Mary. Willingly would I give the ring to be able to make good the wrong which we have done them.'

"'But,' said I, 'by what singular chance

came the ring to be carried into the nest at the top of the tree?

" 'I can soon explain that to you,' said the old huntsman, Anthony, with tears in his eyes, so great was his joy at seeing your innocence acknowledged. 'Neither the old gardener Jacob, nor his daughter Mary, could have hidden the ring in this place; that is very clear. The tree was too high for either of them to have climbed to its summit, where the nest was. Besides, there was not time for them to have done it. Mary had scarcely returned to the house, after leaving the castle, when she and her father were both arrested. But magpies are well known for their liking for anything that is bright and sparkling; and if they come across light articles of the kind they immediately steal them. They carry them off to their nest. Doubtless one of the birds stole the ring and carried it to the tree. That is very plain. The only thing that astonishes me is, that an old huntsman like myself should not have thought before that the birds might have stolen the ring. But it must have been the will of God to send this great trial to my old friend Jacob and to his daughter Mary.'

" 'Anthony,' said my mother, 'you are perfectly right, and the whole thing is now quite clear to me. I recollect distinctly that these birds very often flew down from the top of the old pear-tree on to the window-sill—that the sash was up when the ring disappeared—that the table upon which I had put the ring was close to the window—and that, after having shut the door and bolted it, I went into the next room, where I stayed for some time. Beyond doubt one of the mischievous birds spied the ring from the top of the tree, and took advantage of the few minutes I was in the adjoining room to seize and carry it off unperceived to his nest.'

" My father was much troubled and distressed on seeing such complete and unexpected proof brought to light of your and your father's unjust condemnation.

" ' It pains me to the heart,' he said, ' that so great an injury should have been done to these good people. My only consolation is, that it was not done through ill-will but in ignorance and error. I shall never be able to rest in quiet upon my pillow until these poor people have been found, their innocence proclaimed to the world, and some atonement made for the injustice they have suffered.'

" Thereupon he turned to Juliette, who stood, pale and trembling, more like a condemned criminal than anything else, while all around were rejoicing that an injustice had been brought to light.

" ' You false and deceitful creature!' he cried, ' what can have induced you to lie to your master and to the judge, and thus lead us to do an action the iniquity of which cries to heaven? How could you be so wicked as to bring such cruel and undeserved suffering upon an old man and his poor and innocent daughter?

" ' Arrest her this instant!' he said, turning to a couple of constables, who had assisted in cutting down the tree, and who had already approached Juliette, watching my father the while in anticipation of the command he now gave. ' Let her be loaded with chains,' said he, in a grave tone—' the same chains that Mary bore, and let her be thrown into the same prison in which she caused Mary to languish. She shall suffer all that Mary so undeservedly suffered. All that she possesses, whether in money or clothes, shall be taken from her, to serve as a compensation, if that is still possible, to the unhappy people whom she has caused to suffer

so unjustly. Lastly, the same officer who conducted Mary and her father out of my dominions
shall also conduct Juliette, just as she is, over
the borders.'

" These words made everyone present tremble.
They were all pale and silent. No one had ever
seen my father so exasperated; never had they
heard him speak with so much warmth. A profound silence reigned for some time. But when
at length he went into the castle everyone spoke
his sentiments and thoughts.

" ' It is well done,' said the officer, taking
Juliette by the arm. ' He who digs a grave for
another invariably falls into it himself.' ' That
is what is gained by telling falsehoods,' said the
other officer, taking her other arm. ' Truly says
the proverb, no thread is so fine that it cannot
be seen in the sunshine.'

" ' It was a pretty dress given to Mary,' said
the cook in her turn, ' that made Juliette angry.
In her passion, not knowing well what she was
about, she began to tell falsehoods, and then it
was impossible to retract without acknowledging
herself an infamous liar. Thus the proverb is
not wrong which says, " When once Satan has
got us by the hair, he will lead us to destruction ".'

" ' We can't say but she has been served rightly,' said the coachman, who had been one of those to put the axe to the root of the tree, and who still held the instrument over his shoulder. ' Let us hope that at least this time she will mend her ways, if she does not wish to be worse off in the next world. The tree that bears not good fruit,' said he, shaking his axe, ' shall be cut down, and cast into the fire.'

" The news of the finding of the ring quickly spread through all Terborg, and every one ran to the place to inquire as to the truth of the report, so that in a little while quite a crowd was collected. Amongst others came the magistrate who tried and condemned Mary and her father. His clerk had heard of the discovery, and hastened to tell him of it.

" You can scarcely imagine, my dear Mary, the effect that this story produced on the good man; for notwithstanding his severity towards you, he is most assuredly a man of great honour and probity, and has been distinguished all his life for his fidelity to truth and the rectitude of his conduct.

" ' I would give half my fortune,' he said, in a tone that went to the heart of all present, ' nay,

I would willingly have given everything that I possess, that this had not happened. It is a terrible thing to condemn an innocent person unjustly.' Then, looking round him at the assembled people, he said, in a loud and solemn voice, 'God is the only judge who never errs, and whom no one can deceive. He, the Omniscient, alone knew how the ring disappeared. He alone knew the place in which it has remained hidden until now. The judges of the earth are very liable to err through short-sightedness. Here on earth, unfortunately, innocence must often suffer and guilt come off victorious. But God, the invisible Judge, who will one day judge all hearts, and reward the good and punish the wicked, has in this case been pleased to clear the innocent and make manifest the guilty. And behold how wonderfully circumstances have combined to work out his holy will. It was necessary that this dreadful storm, which shook the whole castle and made us all tremble last night, should bend the old tree until it was ready to fall. It was necessary that a heavy and sudden shower should wash the inside of the nest clean, so that the ring might sparkle and thus attract attention. Then it was necessary that the Count and his family should be at the castle, and that they should come out into the garden to witness the cutting down of the tree. And see, again, with what wisdom it was ordained that the ring should be discovered by the two innocent and frolicsome boys, the young counts, to whom it could not occur to hide it. And then Juliette herself, the false accuser, was the first to make known Mary's innocence by the piercing cry she uttered upon seeing the ring.

" ' This,' the venerable magistrate continued, ' though a surprising, is by no means an extra-ordinary development of events. If we were to observe closely we should often see things as wonderful as the result of the divine providence. In the world to come God will once more take up and retry all the cases in which men have been judged in this world, and will give justice to each according to the right, whether the verdict be eternal death or life everlasting in the heavens. Yet sometimes, even in this world, he so orders events that men are compelled to look up to him, the great Judge who sees all things, and whom none can deceive, and that, notwithstanding the many unrighteous deeds that are done on earth, we may not lose faith in an eternal, all-directing Omnipotent Power, who rules everything in truth and righteousness.'

" Thus spoke the magistrate with much solemnity and impressiveness. Every one listened to him with great attention, and, when he had ceased, dispersed quietly to their homes, deeply moved by what he had said. So now, dear Mary, I have told you the whole story of the finding of the ring and the establishment of your innocence."

By this time the young Countess and Mary had reached the gate of the castle.

CHAPTER XVIII

The Count, the Countess, and the other guests staying at the old hunting-lodge were assembled in the drawing-room, which was decorated with taste and even magnificence, in accordance with the fashion of the olden times. The walls were hung with tapestry, upon which were depicted scenes from the chase, with the huntsmen, horses, dogs, stags, and wild boars, all so life-like and true to nature, that at the first glance, and especially at night when the room was brilliantly lighted with scores of candles, one seemed to be in the glades of the forest itself, so fresh were the colours and so artistic the work.

The worthy pastor had been some time at the lodge, and all the company had listened with great interest to what he had been saying of Jacob and Mary. He had told the story of the pious old man with so much feeling that all were greatly moved. He also gave numerous instances of the filial piety of Mary, of her indefatigable activity, of her patience and modesty, and of the loving care and attention with which she had attended her father to the last. Tears filled the eyes of all who listened to him.

At this moment the Countess Amelia entered the drawing-room, holding Mary by one hand, and with the other carrying the basket of flowers. Every one vied with each other in welcoming Mary, who was overwhelmed with greetings and congratulations.

The Count took her kindly by the hand, and said, " Poor child, how pale and thin you look! It was our inconsiderate conduct that deprived your cheeks of their fresh colour, and furrowed with wrinkles your brow which was formerly so smooth. We will spare no pains in order that the faded flowers may once more bloom on your cheeks. We chased you from your paternal roof; you shall have the house in future for your pro- perty. Your father enjoyed the pretty house and garden at Terborg as a tenant only, but now it shall be yours. My secretary shall make out a deed of gift, and Amelia, who loves you so dearly, shall convey the gift to you with her own hands."

The Countess kissed Mary, pressed her to her heart, called her her daughter, and taking from her finger the ring which had caused so many misfortunes—"Here, my dear child," she said, "your piety is a jewel more precious, it is true, than the large diamond which sparkles in this ring. Still, although you possess a richer treasure, accept this present—receive it as a feeble compensation for the wrong which you have suffered, and as a token of the sincere attachment and maternal tenderness which I feel towards you. If the time should ever come when the price of the ring would be of more value to you than the jewel itself, come to me and I will redeem it from you at its full value."

With these words the Countess put the ring on Mary's finger.

Mary, who had shed so many bitter tears, now shed very sweet ones. She was quite overcome with the kindness shown to her, and was ready to sink under the weight of her sudden change of fortune, as though it was a heavy burden. She could scarcely speak for tears, but she implored the Countess not to ask her to take so rich a treasure.

"Poor child," said one of the two strangers, "take what a generous benefactor offers you. God has blessed the Count and his wife with the good things of this world, but he has given them also something still more precious—hearts which know how to make the best use of their riches."

"Why do you flatter us?" said the Countess. "This is not a generous action—it is but an act of justice. We were the means of doing a great wrong to our poor friend, and it is only an act of Christian duty to undo that wrong and make compensation for it as far as we can."

Mary, always modest, held with a trembling hand the ring which she had taken, and turned her eyes, wet with tears, towards the pastor, as though to ask him what she should do.

"Do not hesitate to accept the ring, Mary," said the venerable minister. "It is the wish of the Count and Countess that you should. As the great trial through which you passed affords an instance of how what seems to be the most circumstantial evidence may lead to error, in the same way let this gift serve as a bright example of the way in which truly noble and upright minds endeavour to make amends for faults they have unknowingly committed. You see, my good child, God is blessing your filial piety; for whoever sincerely honours his parents shall be the better for it. God has promised it, and God makes use of the benevolent hand of the Count and Countess to fulfill his word. Receive, then, their present with gratitude, and since adversity has found in you a due resignation to the divine will, you have only to show yourself in prosperity equally submissive to his will, and ever benevolent and kind."

Mary put the ring on her finger; her tears choked her utterance and expressed her gratitude. Amelia, who stood beside her with the basket of flowers in her hand, was delighted with the generous proceeding of her parents. Her eyes beamed with affection for Mary.

The minister, who had only too often observed how envious children frequently are when their parents exercise their benevolence towards other people, was all the more touched by the disinterestedness shown by Amelia. "May God," said he, "reward the generosity of the Count and Countess, and may all that they have done for a poor orphan be rendered to them a hundredfold, in the person of their own dear daughter. And be sure He will," he added after a pause; "for whatever of our worldly goods we devote to the good of our suffering fellow-creatures becomes pure gain to us.   Not only are we rewarded in this world for our good deeds, but we are thereby, as we are told, laying up treasures in heaven which neither moth nor rust can corrupt, nor thieves take away."

CHAPTER XIX

FURTHER WONDERS OF PROVIDENCE

Supper being now announced, the Countess invited the worthy pastor to remain, and said that Mary also must be of the party. While grace was being said, that beautiful custom being then still observed among the higher ranks of society, Mary's feelings almost overcame her, as she breathed a prayer of thanks-giving to the Almighty for his goodness. She could not help contrasting the position in which she now found herself, with a sumptuously-spread table before her, and what she had frequently of late experienced at Pine Farm, when she had often been obliged to go to bed hungry after a hard day's work. "How I thank thee, Lord, for thy loving care! Forgive my timidity, and give me thy grace, so that I may never more show any lack of confidence in thee!"

Mary was shown to a seat between the Countess and her daughter; but she modestly held back and declined to take that place of honour. But the Countess said with a kindly smile: "Since you, our—not lost, but repulsed—daughter, have been restored to us, it is fitting and proper that we should hold a feast, and at it you are entitled by right to the first place." Saying which she took Mary by the hand and led her to her seat.

During the meal little else was spoken of but Mary's story. The Count had brought with him the honest old huntsman Anthony. This faithful retainer, as much from pleasure as from duty, invariably assisted in waiting at his master's table. This evening he stood almost all the time behind Mary's chair, and from time to time wiped a tear from his eyes. By reason of his age and long service, he was often indulged to the extent of being allowed to mingle in the conversation. He now said, respectfully addressing Mary, " Has it not proved true what I told you and your father in the forest, namely, that honesty lasts the longest, and that he who trusts in God may be sure of divine protection? If your father, the friend of my youth, had lived to see the light of this joyful day, what happiness it would have been for him to see the dearest object of his love on earth proved to all the world to be innocent, and thus covered with honour. Why did he not live to see this day, and taste so great a pleasure?"

" Good old man," said the clergyman, " I admire your sentiments, for they do honour to your heart. But our view must not be limited by the short horizon of this life; it is the smallest portion of our existence: this world is only the vestibule to another. The life we live upon earth is only the preparation for a better one, which is reserved for us in heaven. Now, if we consider the existence of man without regarding his future destination, we shall make a great mistake; but let us raise our eyes to heaven, and then such views will offer themselves to us as will console our minds respecting every dispensation. That was the case with Mary and Jacob. The misfortunes that our young friend endured have been already recompensed in a most noble manner. As for her father, it seemed good to God that he should be plunged into the depths of misery, and die misjudged. But there is another and a better life; there is, happily for us, a celestial dwelling-place. It is there—it is in heaven that the good man is rewarded for all his sufferings—it is there he tastes the joys and the sweets of a glorious existence; and we who are seated at this banquet, in this brilliant room, have not a shadow of the pleasure which he enjoys. But let me relate a fact which I had almost forgotten among so many other things.

"I went one morning to his bed-side. Whatever was his confidence in divine providence, he could not help expressing some anxiety respecting his dear daughter; but that day I found him uncommonly cheerful; his countenance was serene, and there was a smile upon his lips. He held his hand out to me, and said, ' Now, sir, I am at last freed from the burden that was on my heart—my anxiety concerning my daughter; I am now perfectly tranquil. Last night I prayed with more fervour than I ever did in my life, and I felt in my heart the sweetness of a calm unknown until now, and a consolation truly divine. I felt firmly confident that my prayer would be heard. I shut my eyes and slept quite composedly, for I know that the innocence of my daughter will be discovered—the noble Count will take care of her as a father, and she will find a mother in the Countess.'

"Such were the words of the pious old man; and this evening I have learned, to my great astonishment, that it was that very night that the violence of the wind blew down the old tree which grew in the garden of the castle, and thus showed

to the world, with the discovery of the ring that
was lost, the innocence of Mary. Thus, even at
the very moment, was his fervent prayer answered. It is a consolation to me to think that,
even beyond the tomb, he is not a stranger to
the happiness of his daughter, the object of so
much tenderness, and that he participates in our
joys. One thing is certain, that the prayer of this
pious old man, offered up that night, and immediately answered, enlightens this chain of events
with a light which rejoices the soul. It appears
to make this little history a work of divine providence.

" No," continued the pastor with emotion,
" our meeting here is not the effect of accident;
it is not a blind chance which has prepared this
touching scene, which has filled us with so much
happiness. It is the goodness of God—it is his
holy providence which has conducted me, a
stranger, into the midst of this company. He has
willed that I should bear witness of him in reveal-
ing a circumstance confided to me by the dying,
and which has caused us to penetrate into the
secrets of this history. May we be convinced by
this event that God overrules all things. May all
here be persuaded to rejoice in the belief that we

have on high a Father whose paternal heart beats with love for us all. For this belief is our only real comfort in tribulation and death—against the assaults of which no rank is privileged—against which no patent of nobility and no crown is a protection."

"That belief, my dear pastor," said the Countess, rising, and giving him her hand, "I share with you."

Everyone present confessed to holding the same views, and thanked the venerable pastor for giving expression to them.

All had now risen from the table.

"It is getting late," said the Countess, "and as we have to set out very early to-morrow morning, we must rest a little. We will therefore part for the present, in order to avoid any distraction which might make us lose the good feelings which the pastor has awakened in us. We could not finish the day in a better manner."

All then bade each other good night, with hearts full of gratitude to God.

CHAPTER XX

The next morning, as soon as the sun was up, everybody in the castle was busily occupied in making preparations for their intended departure; but busiest of all were the Countess Amelia and the young lady who was on a visit to the hunting lodge with her father, both of whom were doing their utmost to put Mary in a fit state to travel.

Mary had been used to dress as it was customary for those in the service of the gentry to do; but as during her residence at Pine Farm she had been obliged to buy her own clothes, she was able to get only those of the coarsest description, and she was therefore dressed almost exactly as the peasant girls of the neighbourhood.

But the young lady, who was of the same age and size as Mary, presented her, at the request of Amelia, with a complete dress, neat, handsome, and new, and such as, without being at all extravagant, suited her new situation. "For," said Amelia, "henceforth you are my friend, my companion, and you will always live with me; therefore you must no longer dress like a country girl. It is also best that you should change your old clothes for the new here; by so doing you will attract the least attention."

Mary could not do otherwise than yield her consent, though it was at first a reluctant one. She would rather have retained her peasant dress. With the help of her kind young friends the transformation was soon made, and then the two young ladies descended with her to the breakfast-room.

At first every one was astonished to see three young ladies enter the room, but when they recognized Mary they hastened to congratulate her on the improved appearance she made in her new dress. After breakfast the carriage was ordered, and the whole party set out for a drive, Mary being seated beside Amelia, opposite to the Count and Countess. The Count ordered the coachman to take them at once to Pine Farm, as he wished to become acquainted with the people who had treated Mary and her father so kindly. On the way he inquired about their situation with great interest, and Mary did not hide from them that they were far from happy, and that any prospect they had of enjoying anything like comfort in their declining years was very remote.

The arrival of the carriage caused not a little stir at the cottage; for never since the existence of the farm, perhaps, had a carriage—at least never so grand a one—appeared before its door.

No sooner had the young farmer's wife seen the carriage draw up, than she hastened out, saying that she must help the gentleman and lady and their two daughters to alight. Holding out her hand to one of the young ladies, she suddenly recognized her to be Mary herself, and with an exclamation of surprise she let go her hand as if she had touched a serpent, drew back, and turned red and white by turns.

The old farmer was working in his garden. The Count, the Countess, and Amelia went to him, took him by the hand, and thanked him for his kindness to Mary and her father in the warmest terms.

"Ah!" said the honest peasant, "I owe that good man more than he ever owed me. The blessing of heaven came with him into our house, and if I had followed his advice in everything,

I should have been much better for it at this moment. Since his death I have no pleasure in anything but this garden. It is, besides, to his wise advice that I am indebted for reserving this little corner of ground, and from him I learned to cultivate it. Since I have not had strength to follow the plough, I have occupied myself here, and I seek among the herbs and flowers the peace that I no longer find in my house."

Meanwhile Mary had gone to look for the old farmer's wife in her little room, and she now came out into the garden, leading her by the hand, and desiring her not to be alarmed, for the good woman was quite overcome. She approached with a timid and embarrassed air, and was distressed to find herself overwhelmed with thanks.

The good old people were very much confused, and cried for joy like children. At last the farmer, addressing Mary, said, "My dear Mary, did I not tell you that your filial piety would receive its reward? Well, now is my prophecy fulfilled!"

Meanwhile the old woman, who had become a little encouraged by the kindness of the Count and Countess, said, as she ran her hand over

Mary's dress, " Yes, yes! your father was right with his saying—' He who clothes the flowers well knows how to take care of you '."

Their ill-natured daughter-in-law stood at some distance and said to herself, " Well, well! what will not happen in this life? This miserable beggar—now look at her!—she is a young lady of high rank. Who would have thought of such a thing? There is not a woman in our town who can compare with her now. But every one knows who she is—they know that yesterday she set out from here with her little package under her arm, to go and beg about the country."

The Count, of course, did not hear this abusive language, but he was disgusted with the mocking look and angry mien of the woman. " That is a wicked creature," he said; and he walked up and down the garden for some minutes in deep thought. At last, stopping before the farmer, he said, " Listen, my good old man, I have a proposition to make to you. I have given Mary the little piece of ground which was cultivated by her father. But Mary is not yet ready to go into housekeeping. What is there to prevent you from going to live there? It will suit you, I am certain; and I know that the owner will not exact any rent from you. You can there cultivate as you choose herbs and flowers; and, above all, you will find in that pretty abode both rest and peace in your old days."

The Count's wife, the Countess Amelia, and Mary, insisted that the old people should accept this offer. But there was no need of persuasion; for they were happy to be taken from their present uncomfortable situation. At this moment the young farmer came home from the fields, and was anxious to know what had brought to his farm a carriage drawn by four white horses. The moment he knew what was proposed he consented to it, although it cost him a great deal to part with his old parents. His greatest grief had been to see them so badly treated by their own daughter-in-law, and it was a great consolation for him to think that they would be happier. The young wife was delighted at the prospect of getting rid of the old people, whose food she begrudged, and said with an attempt at politeness, " It is most awfully kind of your excellence, and it would show great rudeness on our part if we did not accept your kindness. They are very difficult people to get on with, and they will, I am sure, be best by themselves. Indeed, it is a piece of great good luck for them to have such a chance!"

In his gratitude at seeing his parents so kindly provided for in their old age, the young farmer said, turning to his wife, " Did I not always tell you that to show kindness to the poor brings blessings upon a house and happiness to its inmates? You would never believe it, however; although now perhaps you will confess that I was right."

The ill-natured wife flushed red with anger on hearing these words. She suppressed her rage, however, in the presence of the Count and Countess, but cast so black a look at her husband that he knew he would have to pay for his speech after they had gone.

The Count promised to send for the aged couple as soon as the necessary arrangements could be made to receive them in the cottage at Terborg, and after wishing them and their son and daughter-in-law a good day, the party resumed their seats in the carriage and drove away.

CHAPTER XXI

A CONTRAST

The noble Count did not fail to keep his word. In the autumn a carriage was sent from Terborg to Pine Farm to bring the two old people. The son wept bitterly when he saw that he was going to lose his father and mother. The daughter-in-law, however, who had counted the days and hours until the moment of their departure, felt the keenest joy at the prospect of being at last quite rid of them. But it was soon seen that her joy was not to be altogether unalloyed. Before leaving, the coachman presented her with a legal document, ordering her husband, under penalty of a fine, to pay regularly every quarter a certain amount for the support and maintenance of his parents.

On reading this document, perceiving what it meant, the woman became violently angry. "We have been overreached after all," she exclaimed. "If they had stayed here it would not have cost us half so much to keep them!" She stormed and threatened, and bade her husband not let the old people go. But though he dared not say anything, the young farmer was secretly glad at the turn things had taken. He took good care, however, not to show his joy. The good people set off in the carriage the next morning, followed by the blessings of their son, and the secret maledictions of their daughter-in-law.

This wicked woman had the fate which her conduct towards her parents deserved, and which is always the lot of avarice and inhumanity. She had placed her money in the hands of a merchant who had just set up a manufactory, and who had promised to pay her ten per cent interest. The annual interest was added to the capital, which produced a new interest, and so on each year. The farmer's wife thought herself the happiest of women, and had no greater pleasure in the world than to make calculations of the sum to which all this money would amount in ten and in twenty years. But to all these happy dreams soon succeeded a sudden and terrible reverse. The enterprise of the merchant did not succeed, and his goods were sold by order of the sheriff. This was a thunder-stroke for the farmer's wife. From the moment she heard of this catastrophe she no longer enjoyed any repose. She was seen almost all day either on the road running to see her lawyer or else at one or other of her neighbours', complaining of her hard lot, while she generally spent the night in weeping and scolding. At last, instead of her ten thousand dollars, she received some hundreds. The blow was so severe to the avaricious woman that she gave up to despair; life became a torture to her, and she wished for death. Eaten up with continual cares, weakened and worn out, she was at length attacked with a fever which never left her. Her husband wished to go for the physician of the village, but she would not consent to it. For once the young farmer resisted, and sent for the doctor; but his wife in a passion threw the medicine out of the window, without having even uncorked the bottle.

At last she became so seriously ill that her husband requested the pastor of Erlenbrunn to come and see her. He did so frequently during her sickness, and talked to her in the most per-suasive tones in the hope that she might be induced to repent and amend her ways—to de-tach her heart from the things of this earth, and to turn to God. But this advice made her very angry; she looked at the good minister with utter astonishment.

"I do not know," said she, "for what purpose the clergyman comes to preach penitence to me. He ought to have delivered his sermon to the merchant who defrauded us of our money. As for me, I do not see that I have any great need of repentance. So long as I was able to go out I went regularly to church on Sunday, and at home I never failed to say my prayers every day. I have not ceased to work hard all my life, and I have shown my industry and economy in saving money; nor have I been remiss in regard to the observance of those other virtues which are becoming to a woman. I defy any one to slander me; and among all the poor people who came to my door, not one of them can complain that I sent him away without giving him something. Now I should like to know how any one can behave better? I should have thought that the pastor would have considered me one of the most pious and virtuous people of all his parish."

The venerable pastor saw himself obliged to take a more emphatic tone in order to lead her to amend. He showed her in the most unmistakable manner, that she loved money more than anything in the world, and that avarice, which she wrongly confounded with economy, is in fact nothing but idolatry. He represented to her also that she must number among her sins those transports of anger to which she was so much addicted; that the most lovely of all virtues, filial affection, had totally failed her; that by her greed and avarice she had poisoned the days of her husband, cruelly driven away the poor orphan Mary, and even turned out of her house her husband's aged parents, whom she ought to have cherished and honoured as if they were her own. He convinced her, too, that, with a fortune like hers, she was far from having fulfilled the important duty of charity by having given here and there a small piece of bread or a handful of flowers to a poor man, often merely to get rid of him, and that she knew nothing of true love to man, founded on a sincere love of God. He showed her that the essence of Christianity consists in love to God and men, and that notwithstanding all her boasting of going to church, public worship could not save her soul, for it had never made her any better; and finally, that all her prayers coming from a heart unwarmed by love, were far from being true prayers.

In this direct and pointed way did he find it necessary to talk to her; but when he had gone on for some time she stopped him and refused to listen to him any more. Then she began to sob and cry through passion.

The good pastor, quite troubled, took his hat and cane and went away. " Alas!" said he " how difficult it is for a heart set upon the things of this world to look forward to those of heaven! How far is such a heart from the kingdom of God! It considers itself excused before God by the repetition of a few vain words, and thinks its duty towards its neighbour is performed by throwing to the poor a few superfluous crumbs. Thus people remain incorrigible, and go so far in their blindness as to mistake vice for virtue. Alas!" said he, in passing near the garden and looking at it, " how wrong some people are in supposing that to be rich is to be happy! This farmer's rich wife, with all her money and all her goods, never had in her life one of those happy hours which were bestowed in such rich plenty on poor Mary amidst the flowers of this garden."

However, the farmer's wife had yet much to suffer. She spent whole nights in coughing.

Her avarice was so great that she scarcely allowed herself the proper remedies or nourishment. Nor were her sufferings mitigated by any consoling thought; she was utterly unwilling to resign herself to God, and to submit to the divine will. The good pastor tried in every imaginable way to bring her to a better frame of mind. Occasionally she appeared a little softened during the last days of her life, but she never evinced any true repentance. At last she died, in the flower of her age, a deplorable instance of the effects of avarice, and passion, and love of the things of this world.

CHAPTER XXII

A LATE REPENTANCE

After a while Mary went with the family of the Count to the city in which he resided part of the year. While there a clergyman, whose white hairs betokened his advanced age, came one morning to the residence of the Count, and asked to see Mary. He told her he came from a person who was very ill, probably near to death's door, and who desired to speak with her before she died. He added that the person could not die in peace, unless this favour was granted her, and that she was not willing to speak with any one except Mary herself.

This strange request astonished Mary very much; she consulted the Countess as to what she ought to do. The Countess, who knew the clergyman to be a pious and prudent man, advised her to go with him. At the request of the clergyman, old Anthony accompanied them.

They had a long way to go, the part to which the clergyman led them being in a remote district of one of the suburbs. At length they arrived in front of a house situated in a bye-street, which presented the most gloomy appearance. There were five flights of stairs to mount, the two last of which were so dark, so narrow, and so broken, that Mary was almost overcome with fear.

The clergyman stopped before a door formed of unplaned planks roughly nailed together. "This is the place," said he; "but wait a little."

He went in for a moment, and then returned for Mary, who was shown into a most miserable garret. The window was narrow and dark, and the panes were filled with paper. A broken truckle bed covered with a straw mattress, a broken chair, and a stone pitcher with neither handle nor cover, composed the furniture. The patient stretched on the bed was truly a frightful object. Mary thought she saw a skeleton move and begin to speak with a frightful voice, which resembled the death-rattle more than anything else. The skeleton extended to her a hand which seemed nothing but skin and bone.

Mary trembled in every limb, and it was with great difficulty that at last she learned, by the indistinct words pronounced with difficulty, that this sad spectacle was—Juliette!—Juliette, who, at the castle, had been the cause of all her distress. This wretched woman had learned from the minister that Mary was in the city with the family of the Count; and she wished to see her to ask her pardon for the wrong she had done her. She had begged the clergyman not to mention her name, being afraid that Mary, justly irritated, might refuse to come.

Mary was affected even to tears. She assured Juliette that all, absolutely all, was forgiven a long time ago, and that the only feeling she experienced was the deepest and most lively pity.

"Alas!" said Juliette, "I am a great sinner; I have deserved my fate. Forgetfulness of God —contempt of good advice—the exclusive love of dress, of flattery, and of pleasure, was the first source of my misery, and this it is which has brought me so low. I die the victim of my follies. Oh!" she cried, raising her voice to a pathetic wail, and weeping bitterly, "I fear a still more dreadful fate awaits me in the world to come! You have deigned to pardon me—you whom I so cruelly injured; but I feel the weight of God's displeasure settling on my soul."

Mary had a long conversation with Juliette, and endeavoured to turn her to the precious Saviour, who would receive her if she would repent; but she was obliged to leave her without being satisfied as to her state of mind; and the idea of the sinful Juliette perishing without hope continually weighed on her mind, and affected her spirits. The sad appearance of the once beautiful girl was ever present to her thoughts. Then she recollected her little apple-tree in blossom withered by the frost, and what her father had said to her on that occasion; the most consoling words he had said on his death-bed also presented themselves to her mind, and she renewed the promise which she had made to God, to live entirely to his glory. She remembered the words of our Saviour, " Do good to them that hate you, and pray for them who despitefully use you and persecute you ".

Under these feelings she implored the Countess to relieve Juliette's distress. The generous lady sent her medicine, food, linen, everything indeed of which she stood in need. But it was all too late. At the age of twenty-three she died, a miserable evidence of the folly and wickedness of doing injury to others to promote what we absurdly suppose our own advantage. She gave no evidence of repentance, but died as she had lived—without God, and without hope.

CHAPTER XXIII

MARY'S RETURN TO TERBORG

The next spring, when the country was covered with verdure and flowers, the Count, accompanied by his wife and daughter, returned to the castle. Mary accompanied them, and took her accustomed place in the carriage by the side of Amelia. Towards the evening, as they approached Terborg, and Mary caught sight of the tower of the church all aglow in the light of the setting sun, the gleaming windows of the castle, and her father's house, she was so deeply moved that she could not restrain her tears. "Ah!" she exclaimed, "when I left here how little I expected ever to return, and least of all in such joy and honour! How mysterious are the ways of God, and how good he is!"

When the carriage drew up at the door of the castle, all those in service of the Count, not only the servants, but the higher officials connected with the estate, were drawn up in readiness to receive the family with all due ceremony and respect.

Mary had a most flattering reception. Every one evinced the greatest joy at seeing her again, and congratulated her on the marvellous and providential establishment of her innocence. The old judge who had condemned her took her hand with paternal tenderness, and asked her pardon in the presence of all present for the part he had taken in her condemnation and punishment. He at the same time expressed his gratitude to the Count and Countess for the nobleness of their conduct in endeavouring to make reparation for the injustice committed, and assured them that he had to reproach himself with this misfortune more than any one, and that he was only too anxious to do all in his power to pay the debt he had unwittingly incurred.

The following morning Mary rose very early; she was awoke partly by joy and partly by the joyous light of the sun, which shone brightly into her chamber. She hastened to visit the beloved house in which she was born, and to look once more upon the garden in which she had spent so many happy and profitable hours. On her way she met none but friendly faces;

many of them belonged to young people to whom in their infancy she had been in the habit of giving flowers, but who had grown so much that she hardly knew them.

The old farmer and his wife, who had now been established in the house for some time, came out to meet her, kissed her affectionately, and told her how happily and contentedly they lived. Tears of joy were in the farmer's eyes. "When you were without a home," he said, "we received you under our roof; and now that we are turned out of our own house, you give us this beautiful cottage in which to spend our declining days."

"Yes," said his wife, "it is always best to be hospitable and kind to others; we know not how soon they may be in a position to help us in return."

"That is true," answered the old man, "but we did not think of that then, and were not influenced by such a thought. However, it is not the less true that if we do good to others, we shall always find some to do good to us."

Mary entered the house. The sight of the room—the place where her father used to sit— awoke in her breast sad recollections. She walked round the garden. She had a kindly greeting for every tree planted by her father, as though in each one she saw again an old acquaintance; but she stopped particularly before the little apple-tree, then all covered with beautiful blossoms. "Alas!" said she, "of what short duration is the life of man on earth! He dies, and the trees and shrubs survive him."

Finally she made her way to the arbour where she had passed so many happy days with her father. As she sat there and looked round the garden which he had cultivated in the sweat of his brow, it almost seemed as though she could see him going to and fro as of old. The tears streamed from her eyes at the recollection; but one thought calmed and soothed her heart: it was, that he inhabited a happier abode, where he reaped the harvest of the seed he had sown in this world.

Mary remained as companion to the young Countess Amelia, and each spring returned with the Count's family to spend a few weeks at Terborg, where she was honoured and beloved by every one. One morning she and Amelia were busily engaged in their little work-room finishing a dress; for though the Count was a rich man,

he had not allowed his daughter to grow up in
idleness, considering it the duty of all to occupy
their minds with some kind of work. While thus
employed they were greatly astonished to receive
a visit from the old judge. It was evident from
the fact that he was dressed in official garb that
his business was of great importance. Amelia
and Mary looked at each other, and wondered
what could be the meaning of this ceremonious
visit. The worthy gentleman did not leave them
long in doubt. After showing his respect to the
young Countess, he said that he had a proposal
of great importance to make to Mary. Although
greatly surprised, Amelia at once rose and left
the room, so that the judge might confer with
her friend alone.

He at once turned to Mary and told her that
he came on behalf of his son Frederick, who
had long admired her for her goodness of heart
and her many other noble qualities, and who
the previous day had informed him of his in-
clination, and his desire, if possible, to make her
his wife. The worthy judge added that, like a
good and obedient son, Frederick had been unwilling to make known his affection to her and
his wish without first obtaining the consent of

his father to do so. This consent he not only gave at once, but gladly undertook to speak to her on his son's behalf, and, with her permission, to lay the matter before the Count and Countess. He went on to say that the union, if it could be brought about, would be doubly pleasing to him because of the wrong he had unwittingly done her. It had been committed, he said, in the discharge of his duty, but that fact had not prevented him from passing many a heavy hour on her account; and if she could see her way to accept the offer he made in his son's name, he should look upon their marriage as in some measure making amends for the injustice he had been the means of inflicting upon her.

Mary's confusion and blushes became deeper and deeper as the judge spoke, and she could not at first command herself sufficiently to answer him. The fact is, that she had long had a secret liking for the young man, who was not only of an excellent disposition, but possessed of great natural ability, which he had improved by diligent study and observation. He was also very good-looking. Since Mary's return they had often met, and from time to time they had talked together in the garden of the castle. From the first she had noticed his liking for her, and it had given her unspeakable pleasure to be thought worthy of the esteem of one of so high a character and such exceptional attainments. But as soon as she perceived that her thoughts were inclining towards him she checked herself, and avoided coming in contact with him as much as possible. She was too modest to think herself worthy of such an alliance, and she desired to spare herself the pain of allowing a feeling to grow in her heart which would only plague and torment her. She had endeavoured, therefore, to think as little of him as possible, and had succeeded to some extent in effacing his image from her memory.

She stammered in reply, while the blushes mounted to her cheeks, that she felt herself greatly honoured by the judge's proposal, but that it had taken her so much by surprise that she must have time to consider the matter. She must also consult the Count and Countess, who had been like father and mother to her.

This was quite enough for the wise judge, who at once took his leave. He was greatly rejoiced; he saw that Mary's affection was with his son, and he had not the least doubt that the alliance would be agreeable to the Count and Countess. Going immediately to them, therefore, he asked their approval of the proposition he had made to Mary.

They were both highly pleased. The Count, who was the first to speak, said, " You bring us a very pleasing piece of news, my dear judge. The Countess and I have often noticed the evident liking that exists between your son and our beloved Mary, and have remarked how well adapted they are to each other. We were careful, however, not to show that we noticed anything. We feared lest our wishes should be construed into a command, which would be highly repugnant to us, believing, as we do, that nothing but the purest love can sanctify marriage. It is, therefore, all the more pleasing to us that our wishes have been fulfilled without any interference on our part."

" I congratulate you with all my heart," said the Countess. " A better daughter-in-law than Mary you could not have, nor your son a better wife. Mary has been brought up in the school of adversity, which is the best of all schools. The best of men have little edges and asperities in their character that need to be rounded off or smoothed down, and this is best done by suffering. Mary has a meek and lowly heart.

She has never been spoiled by flattery. She is the most modest and the most unassuming little body I know; and, what is best of all, she is truly and sincerely pious. She has been trained to industry from her childhood, and no one could know better how to manage a household than she does. As to what are called good manners, she has, during her residence with us in the capital, acquired those graces of person, and that polish of address, which are so necessary in good society, with an ease and rapidity truly surprising. Nor has she lost anything in the process; in her, innocence and beauty are most agreeably combined. Indeed, you will find her in every respect a perfect lady, and your son will be a fortunate man if he marries her."

As soon as the Countess had learned from Mary that she was ready to fall in with the judge's proposal, she began to make the necessary arrangements for the wedding. She took everything upon herself, including the purchase and preparation of the trousseau. It was decided that the bride should be married from the castle, and that the wedding breakfast should be given there. The Countess could not have thrown herself into the affair with more heart if it had been her own daughter who was about to be married.

"How nice it would be," she exclaimed, with a smile, "for Mary to wear the ring—the very ring which caused her so much sorrow—as her wedding ring! What could be more appropriate?"

This accordingly was decided upon. It was also decided that the pastor of Erlenbrunn should be invited to perform the marriage ceremony.

The wedding-day was one of the most festive that had ever been known in the country-side. The whole of the Count's family repaired at the appointed hour to the church, which was crowded to the very door with the people of the village and neighbourhood. None who could possibly get out remained at home; all being eager to do honour to a bride who, though she had suffered imprisonment and chains, had risen to such distinction.

The bride looked the picture of beauty and modesty in her white wreath and veil, whilst the young Countess Amelia was the loveliest of bridesmaids. The old huntsman, Anthony, was present with the rest, and he could not help contrasting the position of the bride, the dutiful daughter of his old friend, with that of Juliette, to whose lodging he had accompanied Mary.

The good pastor referred to Mary's father in the most feeling terms, holding up his method of educating his daughter as a model to parents of the way in which children should be trained to piety and right living. He also pointed to Mary as an example to the young, showing how filial love and obedience are the beginning of all virtue.

The wedding breakfast, which was held in the great hall of the castle, was a magnificent affair, and filled every one with delight. Next to the bride, who sat so modestly, and looked so beautiful, by the side of the handsome bridegroom, the object that attracted the most attention—more, perhaps, than the bridegroom himself—was the basket of flowers, which Amelia had secretly filled with the most beautiful flowers, and placed in the centre of the table. The worthy pastor was especially struck by it, and by the happy forethought of the young Countess in placing it there; and in the little speech which he was called upon to make after the breakfast, he threw out the suggestion that Mary should preserve it as a precious heirloom, to remind her at all times of the increasing goodness and watchfulness of God.

CHAPTER XXIV

THE MONUMENT

Meanwhile the monument which Amelia had promised Mary should be raised to the memory of her father had been finished. It was a very simple and beautiful construction of white marble, with an epitaph in gilt letters. To the name of the deceased, his age, and his double profession of gardener and basket-maker, nothing had been added but these words of Jesus, which certainly deserved to be engraven in letters of gold—" I am the resurrection and the life; he that believeth in me, though he were dead, yet shall he live."

Underneath a skilful workman had cut the figure of the basket, which the Lord had made use of in delivering Mary from her trouble. Amelia had drawn the basket, after it had been filled by Mary's hand with the most beautiful flowers, and the drawing, which was a striking resemblance, was copied by the artist. Beneath the basket was written this text from the holy scripture, " All flesh is grass, and all the goodliness thereof as the flower of the field. The grass withereth, the flower fadeth, but the word of the Lord endureth for ever."

It was with great pleasure that the good pastor of Erlenbrunn, Mary's early friend, had the monument erected on Jacob's grave. It had an imposing effect amid the dark foliage of the pines; and when the rose-tree, growing on the grave, was in bloom, and the green branches were covered with roses, some half open, others entirely blown, bent over the marble, which was of a dazzling whiteness, nothing could be more beautiful. The monument was the most striking ornament of the churchyard, and the chief attraction of the village.

The good clergyman never failed to point it out to strangers who came to the village. Many were those who observed that it was a good idea to put a basket of flowers on the tomb of a man who was at once a gardener and a basket-maker.

"Ah!" the worthy pastor would reply, "it is something better than a good idea. This basket of flowers has a much deeper significance than that. It is not without reason that the people of the village look upon it as the silent record of a most touching story. For the ground upon which we tread has been bathed with many a scalding tear."

Then he would seldom fail to narrate to attentive listeners the history of the basket of flowers, invariably concluding his recital with this grand truth, which the whole story is intended to illustrate, namely, that piety to God and truth towards men shall never fail to triumph over the malice of the worst of foes.

Let the young reader be persuaded that, under all circumstances, it is best to do as Mary did—fear God, speak the truth, reverence your parents, and put your trust in God—and whatever trials and troubles you may have to go through, be assured you will live happily in this world, and die with the sure prospect of eternal glory in the world to come!